OCEAN OF DREAMS

Patricia Hagan

A KISMET™ Romance

METEOR PUBLISHING CORPORATION
Bensalem, Pennsylvania

PATRICIA HAGAN

Patricia Hagan is the New York Times Bestselling author of 22 novels. A former award-winning TV-Radio Motorsports journalist, she and husband, Erik, reside atop a North Carolina mountain with their wire-haired fox terrier, Krystal, three pet raccoons, a possum, a red fox, and several other species of wildlife. She is especially proud of her son, Don, a member of the elite U.S. Navy SEALS.

ONE

Jenny was almost out the door of her office when Joey, the mail-room clerk, called from the opposite end of the hall. "Federal Express, Miss Denton. Just came in." He hurried toward her, waving an envelope.

She turned in his direction at the same time Frank Dabney stepped out of his office. "If you want me to drop you off at the Omni, let's get going. I'm running late, and my wife will kill me if we don't get to her niece's wedding rehearsal on time."

Jenny grabbed the envelope from Joey and crammed it into her tote bag as she hurried behind Frank toward the elevator. With so many people crowded in with them, she was not about to yield to curiosity and open her mail just then. They stepped onto the parking deck, and Jenny repeated her gratitude to Frank, adding, "If it's inconvenient to run me by there, I can always grab a cab."

"No, no problem," he assured her, rushing her along. "Frankly, I envy you people who leave your cars at home and then bum rides. You remind me of people who give up smoking, then bum cigarettes.'' He winked to let her know he was only joking.

"Hey," she fired back at him, laughing all the while, "you know I use public transportation most of the time, and you *did* offer."

"Sure, sure." They reached his car, a Thunderbird, clambered in, and were soon careening out of the deck and into five o'clock Atlanta traffic. "What's this deal again that you're going to?" he wanted to know.

"A Nikon exhibition. All the latest equipment. They're serving drinks and heavy hors d'oeuvres."

"So which are you going for? The cameras or the food?"

"Both," she quipped, not about to confide she was about to make a huge investment in state-of-the-art photographic equipment and intended to do her homework before spending so much money.

"Are you meeting Bryan there?"

Jenny shook her head. Frank knew her fiancé, Bryan Morrow, because they belonged to the same athletic club. "No. I asked him, but he said he had to work late. Doing a brief or something."

"I'm not surprised. He's a hard worker, a real go-getter. I'd hate to go to court and have him on the other side. They say that law firm he works for is one of the busiest in Atlanta. Have they made him a junior partner yet?"

"No, but it probably won't be long."

Frank sang Bryan's praises for a few more minutes, then asked, "When's the wedding? I thought it was set for August, and that's not long off, but Bryan hasn't said anything about it lately. Neither have you, for that matter."

Jenny tensed. That was a touchy subject, one she did not care to discuss. Relieved that the Omni was coming up fast, she pointed, "Just let me out there and I can walk the rest of the way. If you turn off here, you'll miss a lot of traffic."

"Right," he said gratefully, quickly swerving to the curb.

She thanked him again, got out, and headed for the massive building. No way was she about to divulge to Frank—or anybody else, for the time being—that the wedding was going to be postponed. Everyone would want to know why, and she wanted to keep it under wraps for a while that she was leaving Cuisine Unlimited to start her own advertising company. Good grief, it had been bad enough telling her parents and Bryan, because they thought she was out of her mind. Why on earth would she want to do something like that? her father had indignantly challenged. Once she married Bryan, he pointed out, she wouldn't have to work anymore, anyway. *Well, pooh on that idea*, she fiercely reflected. She had no intentions of spending her time on the golf course or going to garden club meetings, or whatever it was that full-time homemakers did these days to keep busy. She liked the pace of the business world and intended to stay in it. Unfortunately, Bryan shared her father's negative opinion, but he was just going to have to get used to the idea of her having a career of her own.

She stood on the corner, waiting for the light to change, and watched the people surging out of high-rise office buildings. One day, perhaps she *would* want to stay home, raise a family, but *she loved* it out there—the challenge, the intense competition. Maybe, too, she reflected, starting her own company was doubly exciting because it was the first real decision she had ever made on her own. Looking back, she felt as programmed as the office computers. Punch in a program and Jenny does this. Insert a new disk and Jenny does that. All her life, everything had been decided, even to where she would attend college—the University of Georgia, where her parents had gone, of course. Retired now, they lived in Florida, but she, an only child, still felt their dominating influence in her life.

Like with Bryan, a nagging voice within reminded. From day one, when she took him home to meet them, they had made up their minds he was the right husband for her. Ever since, they had encouraged the romance. Oh, not that Bryan was not wonderful, and she wasn't crazy about him, it was just that, more and more, he seemed a part of the obligatory computer program that had become the core of her existence, so. . . . so damned *programmed.*

The light changed, and Jenny hurriedly crossed the intersection. She entered the Omni by a side door, at once saw a large poster pointing the way to the exhibit, and headed in that direction.

A Susie Wong lookalike handed her a glass of white wine as she walked in; another directed her to a table of stuffed mushrooms and egg rolls. But it was not the food she was interested in—it was the display of photo equipment that captured her attention.

Already she had bought books on all aspects of photography, then signed up for a class three evenings a week at Atlanta Tech. She knew what she was looking for—high-tech cameras, a camcorder and all the accessories, sound and light meters, battery packs, the works. Next, she had visited several printers to get cost estimates on the color brochures and catalogs she envisioned creating herself for her new company. She was not going into her project unprepared.

As she drifted around the room, taking in everything and sipping the wine, she was trembling with excitement. What a venture it was going to be. The idea was born when she realized that, despite her achievements and success, she felt an emptiness in her career. She had moved up the executive ladder at Cuisine Unlimited, joining the Atlanta-based corporation right after graduating with a degree in business administration. The company was dedicated to creating advertising campaigns that would enhance the attraction of the country's rapidly growing fast-food chains. In exchange, Cuisine Unlimited not only got a fat fee but also a percentage of profits. In turn, responsible executives were rewarded with special dividends and stock options for their efforts. Though it was not an easy task to make a greasy hamburger come across as a superlative culinary treat, Jenny was gifted with a flair for creativity, and, in just a short time, had an impressive list of dedicated accounts. She had developed ideas and slogans that took Jetfood from the bottom of the hamburger havens to the top. She also made Prince of Weiners a king-size chain, doubling their number of restaurants within three years, along with Zippy Pizzas, which had only fifteen stores in two states when Jenny took them on, but now boasted thirty-two in five. As a result of her accomplishments, she commanded a six-figure salary, and Cuisine Unlimited had installed its first female-executive restroom and presented her with a gold-plated key.

The only drawback to it all, however, was Jenny's private discontent. After all, Jetfood still produced hamburgers loaded with fat and cholesterol and were nicknamed "gut-bombs" by the diet-conscious. Prince of Weiners was in the same category, and she would personally starve before ever biting into a greasy Zippy Pizza.

What it boiled down to, she supposed, was that while she could take satisfaction in being hailed in the industry as a promotional wizard, she wanted to feel a personal glory. Other than a monetary reward, what was so gratifying about taking a floundering and undeserving food chain and making it prosperous? What it amounted to was brainwashing people. And she did not like that.

Then one day, out of the blue, it came to her: she would start her own professional consulting firm. The more she thought about it, the more excited she became. She would target accounts she felt needed her services, creating proposals for advertising, new images, directions, and goals. The challenge would be in choosing worthwhile business concepts, instead of hustling "greasy spoons," as it were.

She further decided her idea would take off because she would bear the presentation cost herself. When the account was signed, she would ultimately recoup the expense. Of course, there would be those who were not interested, and those losses she would have to absorb. Fortunately, she could afford a few of those and felt confident there would not be many, anyway. Her first target, she had decided, would be the Valhalla Cruise Lines. Last fall, when she and Bryan had taken a cruise to Mexico, she had visited a travel agent to select their ship. Based on the brochures she was given, she had chosen Sea Star Lines, only to wind up very disappointed. Sea Star, it turned out, catered to an older group of passengers, and she and Bryan had felt rather out of place. During dinner at a seaside restaurant one evening, they had, however, met a delightful couple who had sailed into port on one of Valhalla's ships, the *Viking Princess*. Invited on board as the couple's guests, Jenny and Bryan were both delighted and disappointed. They found the ship more suited to their tastes and their stations in life and regretted they had not been aware of it earlier.

So the wheels began to turn in Jenny's innovative mind, and she realized there was a great need for Valhalla to revamp their sales brochures and catalogs. She had written a letter to them, outlining what she would like to do and was waiting anxiously to hear from them.

Suddenly, Jenny nearly choked on the wine she was sipping, as awareness yanked her from reverie. The Federal Express envelope suddenly weighed like a brick in her tote bag.

It had to be from Valhalla!

Pressed in by people, she glanced around, saw the sign pointing to the women's lounge, and quickly made her way in that direction. Once inside, she was relieved to find it empty and, tore open the outer wrappings at once. With heart pounding, she realized she was right—it *was* from Valhalla.

She scanned the lines and felt like screaming with joy. Not only had they liked her idea, they were inviting her to take a cruise at their expense in order to familiarize herself with their largest ship, the S.S. *Misty Seas*. They welcomed her ideas for new promotion of their pride and joy. And the cruise was not just *any* cruise, either. Ordinarily, Valhalla's S.S. *Misty Seas'* itinerary was the Caribbean, but as the letter explained, it was nearly time for annual refurbishing of the huge, lavish ship and Hamburg, Germany, with its large port facilities, could service it. Of Norwegian registry, the ship owners decided to try something different. Instead of merely sailing to Europe for dry docking, Valhalla had concocted a special itinerary—summer cruises up the scenic coasts of Norway, into the majestic fjords and on up to the North Cape before going to Hamburg. And would she be traveling alone, they asked, or would she like to bring a companion?

Then and there, Jenny was so happy she laughed out loud. What a wonderful vacation for Bryan and her, all expenses paid, and she could not wait to tell him about it!

She ran out of the restroom, pausing at the exhibition desk to grab up every available brochure. There would be time later to decide exactly what equipment to order. For the moment, she had to get to Bryan's office and share her wonderful news.

Outside, she spotted a wine shop across the street and went in and bought a bottle of Cristal and a "to-go" pack—glasses, a bucket of crushed ice, cheese, crackers. This was to be a real celebration. First they would toast the future, then fall on his leather couch and make mad, passionate love. He would share her enthusiasm, she feverishly prayed. He *had* to, for what good was happiness and optimism if not shared with someone you cared about?

Loaded down with her purchases, she managed to wave down a cab, jumped in, gave the directions to the law offices of Jenkins, Jenkins, Bigelow, and, she smiled to herself proudly, soon-to-be-added *Morrow*.

The cab pulled up to the curb and she hurried into the building, nodding to the sleepy-eyed doorman as he buzzed her inside. She took the elevator to the fifth floor, humming to herself and willing it to hurry, hurry, hurry. When she stepped off, she did not go to the main door opposite the elevator that entered into the reception room. Instead, she turned and went down a side hallway that led to the private entrance to Bryan's office.

The lock was a combination type, which she knew. She set down her packages, then deftly punched in the numbers. The door immediately swung open to darkness. Thinking Bryan had finished work early and had already gone, Jenny started to leave but hesitated at the surprising sound of heavy, ragged breathing. Curiosity overcoming apprehension, she instinctively reached for the wall switch, flooding the room with light.

On the leather sofa on the opposite side of the room, Bryan was lying naked on top of a woman, who was also naked, and it was only when both turned their heads at the sudden and quite unexpected intrusion that Jenny realized with yet another painful jolt that the woman was her best friend, Linda Lee.

Instead of instant anger and fury, Jenny was struck with the strange thought of how ridiculous people looked when they were having sex, and how she had never contemplated that unpoetic fact. But what difference did it make? Her heart and soul had just been smashed to bits and pieces by two people who had occupied a very special place in her world.

Finally, when no one moved, Bryan managed to make a stammering sound, then, nervously clearing his throat, staying in that absurd position of neither exit nor entry into Linda, whose legs were wrapped around his back. "Uhhh, Jenny, listen. I can explain, believe me . . ."

Linda made a soft, choking sound and turned her face against the back of the sofa.

Jenny took a deep breath, let it out slowly, and from somewhere in her grieving mind found the strength to say, "It doesn't matter, Bryan. Not anymore."

With trembling fingers, she took off the diamond engagement ring he had given her Easter, carefully laid it on his desk, and began to back out. "Just get on with what you were doing," she managed to choke out with a shrill giggle. "That must be a very uncomfortable position for both of you."

She closed the door, turned and ran, fighting to hold back the heart-tearing sobs that burned in her throat.

TWO

The overhead lights dimmed and passengers settled down to watch the in-flight movie. Jenny declined the headphones, since she was much too keyed up to concentrate on a film. Instead, she requested a glass of white wine, smiling at the irony of California vintage on a British Airways flight.

Valhalla had generously booked first-class seats, and she also had one to herself. She was once again glad to have chosen the comfort of the silk jumpsuit for travel. Removing her low-heeled leather Amalfis pumps, she pushed them with her toe beneath the seat in front, next to the Gucci bag. At last she could close her eyes and allow the mental parade to begin, back through the archives of bad memories for one last time. After that, she was determined to look forward, allowing retrospection only for reassurance not to repeat past mistakes.

After walking in on Bryan and Linda having sex (she could not bring herself to call it ''making love!'') Jenny had not gone back to his apartment where she ordinarily stayed during the week. Instead, she had taken a cab to her own townhouse in the suburbs. She now felt like a fool for having entrusted it to the care of Linda Lee back when she and Bryan had become so involved. The first thing she did was angrily yank Linda's clothes out of the closets and throw them on the front porch, along with her makeup and toilet articles.

When the phone had rung, less than ten minutes after she got home, she had known without a doubt it was Bryan and had not hesitated to answer, hissing in response to the familiar sound of his voice, "You bastard!"

"Jenny, you've got to listen! Please!"

He was begging, sounded like he was actually crying. *So what?* "The only reason I answered the phone is to tell you I'll come by tomorrow and pick up my things, and I'll leave your key on the table. And you can tell your new girlfriend her things are out in the yard and I really don't give a damn what happens to them!"

"Listen, Jenny, please. It's not like you think. I mean, it just *happened,* and neither one of us meant for it to. I mean, there was just these vibes between us, and we sort of fell into each other, you know? It hasn't got anything to do with how I feel about you, and—"

"Well, gee, Bryan, it's a good thing I found out now," she was quick to retort sarcastically. "I mean, it would've been terrible after we got married to find out my husband was just *falling* into my so-called best friend any time the urge struck. So how long has all this been going on?" she hotly demanded.

He sounded miserable. "Not that long. A couple of times." Then, suddenly becoming defensive, he accused, "It's *your* fault. You pushed us together. You were always so busy with your night classes, so caught up in starting your own business, so preoccupied with your career that you didn't have any time for me. *She* was there. *You* weren't."

At that, Jenny had exploded. "Well, look around, buster, and make sure she's still around, because I'm ringing off for good!" And she had slammed the receiver so hard the plastic had cracked—$29.95 down the tubes!

She had not heard from Linda, who mysteriously appeared some time during that night to collect her belongings off the manicured lawn of the apartment complex. No doubt Bryan had brought her there, accommodating Lothario that he was!

Jenny had gone to his apartment the next day to get her belongings, after first checking with his secretary to make sure he was indeed in court and would not be home when she got there. She had quickly packed everything, surprised at how she had actually moved in without realizing it, ignoring the note he had left on the table beside a dozen red roses. More roses waited at the office, and she left them with the receptionist, along with the message that if Bryan Morrow called, to tell him she was running away to be a rock-star groupie. The receptionist just looked at her and blinked, wisely making no comment. Jenny was in a terrible mood.

When she left work that day, Bryan had been waiting outside with a pettifogging plea. "Can't we be adult about this, Jenny?" he begged. "I swear it didn't mean anything. *She* didn't mean anything . . ."

Jenny had brushed right by, ignoring him, stifling the impulse to slug him. Then he had made the fatal mistake of trailing after her, telling her she was being immature. All of a sudden she whirled on him and shouted, "Immature? You dare call *me* immature, Bryan Morrow? You egotistical jerk! When you learn to keep your pants zipped, maybe then you can talk to me about maturity! Now get out of my way before I punch you!"

People had turned to stare, and Bryan had shrunk away with a stricken, disbelieving look on his face to disappear in the crowd. Feeling absolutely mortified to have lost control, Jenny had fled in the opposite direction, desperately wishing for a hole she could crawl into.

So, wanting only to escape, she had called Valhalla and told them she wanted to book the cruise as quickly as possible, which turned out to be in two weeks, and *no*, she had crisply informed the agent, she would *not* be traveling with anyone. Then she gave notice at the office, much to everyone's surprise and disappointment. She went shopping, sparing no expense on glamorous clothes. The night before leaving, she mailed the letter to her parents telling them she was off to Europe and Bryan was history. No doubt they would get in touch with him to try to find out what was going on, and she smiled to think of how he would squirm trying to explain to them how immature their daughter was to freak out over literally catching him with his pants down.

So as the jet streaked across the night sky, Jenny was anything but dubious about her journey alone and the upcoming changes in her life. She was excited, confident, and very much determined to put the past behind her. One rotten apple was not going to ruin *her* whole barrel!

And she felt good about herself, too. A trim and curvaceous size eight, toned to perfection thanks to the Nautilus center near her office, she also used her creative flair to present herself stylishly. She wore her strawberry-blond hair in a shoulder-length shag and knew how to enhance her hazel eyes with proper makeup. Men complimented her, and, to be honest, she did regard herself as pretty. So what, then, had turned Bryan to Linda? True, Linda was also attractive, but *she* was the one he professed to be in love with and had wanted to marry. Could it be that Linda was better in bed than she was? But Bryan had always seemed pleased with their lovemaking, and Jenny certainly did not regard herself as being the least bit inhibited. Last year, when they'd had a brief holiday in the south of France, she had not hesitated to peel out of her bikini top to sunbathe bare-breasted and there was not much they had not tried in bed, either. *So what was his problem?* Bryan, she told herself, was just a creep, and two-faced Linda had the morals of an alley cat.

So be it.

She would not look back. Only forward. And she'd be a hell of a lot wiser, too!

Turning her thoughts to a more pleasant subject—the future—she recalled how she had hit upon the name for her new company. She had gone to an exhibit of the newest designs in laser printers, and, at the wine and cheese reception following, she had run into an old acquaintance who praised her latest triumph—Astro Cookies. Jenny took no particular delight in hearing once again how ingenious she was for adding Astro to the offering of cookie shacks in malls. A spinoff of Chinese fortune cookies, they were dry, papery shells wrapped around generic predictions but the gimmick was they were divided into bins according to astrological signs. Gullible people readily forked over a dollar a piece for the tasteless concoction in order to read their daily horoscopes.

The acquaintance had congratulated her by saying, "Jenny, you just have a *flair* for what you do."

And it hit her.

Then and there.

Flair Promotions.

Her company.

Her targets.

Her ideas.

No more greasy hamburgers turned into culinary delights!

She was going to take good businesses and make them better, through innovation and development. And Valhalla Cruise Lines would be her first success.

Finally, she dozed, waking when the stewardess offered a tray of warm, wet washcloths. Cheerily, she asked Jenny if she would like to freshen up before breakfast and landing.

Soon, they were at London's Heathrow Airport, and Jenny made her way to the SAS Airline terminal to continue on her way to Amsterdam.

Then, at last, the plane touched down at the Schiphol Airport in Amsterdam, famed for its shopping concourses. Jenny longed for horse blinders to suppress the desire to pause at each and every window.

But there was little time for window-shopping and even less for shopping. The moment Jenny entered the terminal, she saw the perky-looking girl dressed in a blue-and-white sailor suit. She flashed a practiced smile as she held up a big sign proclaiming, Welcome S.S. *Misty Seas* Passengers.

Jenny joined the group of other passengers who had been on the same plane, feeling like part of a happy herd as they followed their guide to the Customs and Immigration Center to present their passports.

Finally, passport duly stamped, Jenny was about to continue to the boarding area where busses waited to transport passengers to the dock. But then she noticed a young woman about her age standing to one side with tears streaming down her face. She looked so lost and alone that Jenny's heart went out to her, and she hurried over to ask what was wrong.

"My luggage," the girl broke into sobs. "Every piece has been lost." She wrung her hands, in the process dropping her purse.

Jenny retrieved it for her and thought how pathetic she looked although, she was attractive, in a delicate kind of way, with soft brown hair and big cinnamon-colored eyes. "Are you traveling alone?" Jenny asked.

The girl looked terrified as she nodded with a sniff. "And everything was going great till I went to claim my luggage, and it wasn't there."

"Did you make a report?"

She started crying again. "Yes, and they aren't sure it even got to London on the flight from Chicago."

"But they'll find it," Jenny soothed. "They usually do."

"But even if they do, it wouldn't get here before we sail."

The hostess from Valhalla saw them and came over to ask what the problem was. The girl just shook her head, sobbing, so Jenny had to explain the situation.

"When they find it," the hostess said brightly, "they'll send it to the next port to catch up with you. It happens all the time. Not to worry. Now, you girls need to get outside to the loading dock where the busses are waiting to take you to the ship." Flashing what was meant to be a reassuring smile, she hurried on her way.

"Come on," Jenny urged. "There's nothing else you can do. My name's Jenny Denton, by the way. What's yours?"

"Carla Sutton." She sniffed again, lower lip trembling.

"Well, let's go on to the ship. It's not as bad as it seems."

Carla fell into step beside her. "I don't even have a change of clothes," she lamented.

Jenny gave her a sideways look. "Well, we're about the same size. I can loan you something for tonight."

For the first time, hope shone in Carla's eyes. "Really? You don't mind?"

"Hey, we're here to have a good time," Jenny reminded, "and we aren't going to let a little thing like lost suitcases spoil it, are we?"

"If you say so," Carla murmured hopefully.

Jenny realized she felt protective toward Carla, like a big sister. She just seemed so lost, so alone. They boarded the bus, were soon enroute to the pier, and despite her problems, Carla seemed in better spirits since making a friend. When the magnificent ship at last came into view, she gasped in awe and excitedly squeezed Jenny's hand.

The S.S. *Misty Seas* was, Jenny thought, truly beautiful. Deep, dark blue at the waterline, the upper decks were glistening white, the twin smokestacks also capped in blue. But, she reminded herself, it was also a well-kept secret as far as promotion and publicity went, like all of Valhalla's vessels. She would soon change that, she inwardly gloated. Flair Promotions would make Valhalla Cruise Lines a force to be reckoned with in the business world.

Leaving the bus, Jenny and Carla hurried together up the gangplank. In the area known as purser's square, more vivacious girls dressed in sailor suits awaited, eager to give boarding passengers directions to their cabins.

Jenny presented her boarding pass to one of the waiting hostesses, and her reaction was an impressed exclamation of, "Oh, you have one of the Fantasy suites."

At that, Carla squealed, "Oh, we're on the same deck, Jenny. That's where *my* cabin is." She held out her own boarding pass for scrutiny.

The hostess looked at it, then grinned at both women in turn as she jovially declared, "More than that, girls. You're in the *same* suite. Didn't you know?"

"No!" Carla cried, delighted, as she clapped her hands and bounced up and down on her toes in little-girl glee. "Maybe, at last, my luck is changing! Isn't that wonderful, Jenny?"

And Jenny managed to smile, though faintly, wondering what it was going to be like to share a cabin with her suddenly adopted little sister.

________ THREE ________

They sidestepped luggage piled outside stateroom doors. People were milling about, some lost, some just enjoying the confusion and excitement before sailing.

"There's a bon voyage party on the outer decks right before we leave," Carla reminded, stepping out of the way of a porter with a luggage dolly, and eyeing the arriving suitcases with envy. "Do you want to go?"

"Of course I do," Jenny assured. "I think I've memorized the whole schedule, and I don't want to miss anything."

Hurrying to keep up, Carla wailed, "I know I'll get lost. Good grief, they say this ship is longer than three football fields."

"Just about," Jenny mused, glancing at the paper in her hand that explained the ship's layout. "According to this, to get to our suite, we take the elevator up to the Starlight deck, then follow the blue stars in the silver carpet to the section that has red carpet with gold stars. Got that?"

"I'll never remember."

"Sure you will. At the end of two weeks, you'll be a veteran cruiser. So will I . . . as long as I've got this map in my hand!" They both laughed.

At last they stood in front of the Venus suite, a glimmering silver replica of the famous statue almost entirely covering the ornate wood door. Jenny reached for the brass handle and paused to say with a flourish, "Welcome on board, Miss Sutton."

As she swung the door open, they both gasped out loud. "It . . . it's like something out of a movie," Carla marveled. "I . . . I don't believe it."

The carpet was soft and thick, a pale rose color, and the wallpaper was a design of trailing pink and peach-colored roses, amid sea-green ivy. There were white silk drapes at the huge picture window, framing an endless panorama of blue. Twin double beds were covered with white-and-peach spreads, with tufted velvet headboards in a shade to match that of the wallpaper. A small round table was positioned in front of the window, with four leather chairs circling it. There was an entertainment center at the end of the room, complete with television, VCR, stereo, and a wet bar. A bottle of wine was chilling in a crystal bucket packed with ice. Beyond an arched doorway they could see a dressing area and an arrangement of fresh flowers had been placed in there, as well as on the dresser in the main room.

"I just don't believe it," Carla repeated, turning around slowly and marveling at the sublime luxury. "And I only had to pay the same price I would've paid for a lower class."

Jenny raised an eyebrow. "Was that because the ship is fully booked?" she inquired curiously.

Carla nodded. "But wasn't it the same with you?" she wanted to know. "I mean, the only reason they put me in here was because the class I could afford was full. You aren't paying *full price* for all this, are you?''

Jenny saw no need in confiding her fare was complimentary, so instead hedged, ''I guess they either had to take us or sail with this suite empty, and that didn't make sense.''

Since Jenny's luggage had not yet arrived, they decided to explore the ship. As it turned out, they had no sooner circled their own deck before a voice with a distinct foreign accent came from an overhead loudspeaker to remind them sternly that the mandatory lifeboat drill was about to begin. They hurried back to the suite to get the orange vests. Jenny took note of the map on the back of the door directing them to their station and led the way.

A crowd had already gathered along the railing, over which the lifeboat was suspended by ropes, but no one seemed to know what was going on. Jenny wandered over to the railing and quickly became mesmerized by the sight of the rolling sea, a mysterious shade of gray and green in the pale afternoon light. The setting was so peaceful, and she took a deep breath to drink in the crisp salty air.

''It's so pretty,'' Carla said, joining her. ''You know, I still can't believe I'm really here. At first I thought about taking a cruise in the Caribbean, but then I heard about the *Misty Seas* going to Norway, and I said Why not? I need the adventure.''

''What do you do, Carla?'' Jenny probed curiously. ''I mean, where do you work?''

''Oh, when I get back, I'll have to find a job,'' she said with a shrug, as though really not concerned.

Jenny blinked in surprise. ''You mean you don't work?'' Perhaps, she quickly thought, Carla had inherited some money and that was how she could afford the trip.

''Well, I *did,*'' she began to explain. ''Till Robbie and I divorced. We were both hairdressers in our own salon.

He offered to buy me out when we split, and I said okay, because at the time I agreed it was best we didn't work at the same place, and he pointed out how he was willing to give me a fair price, even though he'd done most of the work building up the place. You know, making booths and shelves, things like that.

"And . . ." she went on, pausing for a ragged sigh, "I have to admit to being the world's biggest fool. I guess in the back of my mind, I thought if things went smoothly and I didn't make a hassle, he'd change his mind later and we'd get back together. He even hinted that might happen, that we could go to a marriage counselor even."

"How long were you married?" Jenny interrupted to ask.

"Nearly ten years. No kids, thank goodness. Not that I didn't want any, but I'm just glad now that we never had any because of the way things turned out. Robbie kept saying we needed to build the business, that we could have kids later. Anyway, I found out soon enough we'd *never* get back together, because he got married again before the ink was dry on the divorce decree. He'd been fooling around behind my back, and I was too dumb and blind to see it."

"That happens to lots of people," Jenny wryly commented, then attempted to lift Carla's spirits. "But you got a settlement. You can start over again. Maybe open your own shop."

"Right!" Carla nodded happily. "But first I wanted a real vacation for the first time in my life. Robbie and me, we worked hard all those years. I never even got to go out of town to the style shows. I stayed behind to keep the shop open, while he took the models and went. He won lots of prizes, too. The shop was full of trophies.

"Anyway . . ." She shrugged again, mustered a confident smile. "I'll worry about finding a job, or renting a booth, or whatever, after I get home. For now, I just want to have a good time and not think about the past. At least I ended up with a pretty good settlement.''

''My sentiment exactly,'' Jenny grinned at her, all the while thinking that Carla sounded a little desperate.

''May I have your attention?''

They turned to look at the officer who had spoken.

''Oh, my God, he's gorgeous!'' Carla whispered.

Jenny suddenly found herself staring up into the most beautiful blue eyes she had ever imagined. All at once, she knew the true meaning of ''fjord-blue,'' for this well-proportioned male standing in front of her just had to be Nordic. His hair was blond, not the California variety, but more of a sand color, and natural, smooth. It barely touched the collar of his crisp, short-sleeved white shirt. Epaulets on his broad shoulder denoted his rank of Chief Officer Senior—she remembered that from the cruise information booklet that had been provided with her tickets. His gaze met hers, held momentarily, and Jenny felt an undeniable tremor within. Carla was right. He *was* gorgeous!

He forced himself to look away from the stunning young woman with such lovely hazel eyes. Then, clearing his throat, he introduced himself. ''I am Chief Officer Senior Kirk Moen. Under normal sailing conditions, my duty is to oversee all operations and report directly to the captain. *However*, God forbid . . .'' he paused to flash a smile meant to be reassuring, ''. . . should we have an emergency at sea and forced to abandon ship, you will report, on signal, to this station, where *I* will be in absolute command.''

His gaze fell once more on the young woman, and he found himself thinking how she had the warmest, kindest eyes he had ever seen. She seemed to exude a freshness, a spirit, and he gave himself a mental shake, getting back to the importance of the moment at hand. "Is this understood?" he asked of no one in particular. When there was a general murmur of acquiescence to his authority, he continued. "I have here a list of all cabins and the number of passengers in each who will report to this station. Please answer when I call your name."

He paid particular attention when *she* responded, and when she said her name was Jenny Denton, knew at once who she was—the American woman vying for the Publicity and Promotion contract. He knew they would have business to discuss later but wondered if he could keep things on that level in view of the effect she was having on him.

Roll call completed, he began the usual inspection to make sure everyone's life jacket was fastened properly.

He made the routine adjustments, loosening or tightening. Then he was standing in front of her, saw that she had not wrapped the straps properly beneath the vest. He reached to adjust, felt a rush as his fingers brushed against her breasts. Full. Firm. *Nice.*

At his touch, Jenny experienced a delicious tremor within. Dear Lord! His nearness was overwhelming, making her almost dizzy, and she fought to keep from swaying. His eyes met hers, held, and she could not look away, realizing she did not want to. She did not even mind the knowing curve to his lips, knew he was enjoying the moment as much as she was. Feeling playfully wicked, she took a deep breath, deliberately swelling her bosom even more as she huskily murmured, "I never can get these on right."

He was lingering longer than necessary, enjoying the moment. "You cruise often, do you?"

She wondered what it would be like to hear that sexy accent make pillow talk. "Uh, not really," she was almost stammering, silently commanded herself to calm down. "I went to Mexico last year on the Sea Star Lines."

"Terrible ships," he said bluntly. "That's an Italian line. Italians aren't exactly known for being sailors. Norwegians are."

"And that automatically makes your ships better, right?" she teased.

"Of course," he fired back, liking her spirit and once more thinking what beautiful eyes she had. He gave her strap one last tug, again brushing his fingers across her breasts. "You're okay now. I don't think you'll drown."

Except in your blue eyes, she silently avowed. Chiding herself for acting like a silly schoolgirl, she immediately countered with a silent *So what?* Maybe she had come on the cruise to try to win the contract, but there was no harm in having some fun, especially after what she'd just been through. After all, finding out her fiancé had been making it with her best friend had given her ego a pretty big wallop. Deep down, she still could not help wondering whether Bryan would have "fallen into" Linda, as he called it, had *she* been more sexually interesting. That possibility would subconsciously haunt her, she knew, for a long, long time.

Officer Moen stepped back just as three short blasts of the ship's horn sounded to signal the drill was over.

"Hey, we're moving!" Carla suddenly cried, running once more to the railing.

Jenny turned to follow but not before glancing in *his* direction. She saw that he was walking at a brisk pace toward the front of the ship, heading, no doubt, for the bridge and his command post for sailing.

All around, people were shouting, cheering, making merry as members of the cruise staff passed out helium-filled balloons, bags of confetti, and streamers. From a deck below, a band was playing a lively march tune.

The ship's horn blared again, and more cheers filled the air.

"I can't believe it!" Carla was jumping up and down, tears sparkling in her eyes. "I'm really *here*, Jenny. In *Europe!* And I'm going on a cruise to Norway and I've made a wonderful new friend and I just know lots of great things are about to happen—even if I don't have anything to wear," she added with an embarrassed laugh.

"We'll manage!" Jenny cried, so filled with exuberance and optimism that no obstacle seemed insurmountable.

They hugged each other and cheered and waved and let go of their balloons and tossed confetti and streamers, and then things began to quiet down a bit.

An announcement was made over the PA system that passengers who had not already done so should proceed to the dining room to receive their table-seating assignments.

"We haven't done that," Jenny reminded.

"Do we have to lug these?" Carla was squirming out of her life jacket.

Jenny also removed hers and offered, "If you'll go on down and get in line, I'll take them back to the cabin and meet you there. Try to get a window table."

"I just want to make sure we sit together."

"We will. Can you find your way?"

Suddenly, a young man who had been standing close by stepped up to inquire amiably, "Are you supposed to go to the Athena or the Sea View?"

"I'm not sure." Carla began to dig frantically into her purse in search of her dining assignment card, while Jenny quickly scrutinized the smiling stranger. He was nice-looking, in a practiced kind of way—the *too smooth* hair style, *too smooth* David Letterman outfit—khaki pants, navy blazer, white shirt and tie. Through her years of business travel and stops in hotel lounges for a drink now and then, Jenny had seen his kind too many times, in too many places, and was well aware of his modus operandi—extremely charming, with just the right facial expressions, mannerisms. Charisma. A real operator!

He glanced at her, then blinked in dismissal as though aware she could see right through him, and turned his attention instead on Carla. "My name is Russ Claiborne, by the way."

"I'm Carla Sutton, from Chicago," Carla was quick to respond. "This is my cabinmate, Jenny Denton, from Atlanta. Or maybe I should say we're *suite*-mates. We're in the Fantasy section," she added proudly.

"Oh, really? I tried to book one of those, but they were full. I had to take one of the lower decks instead." He wrinkled his nose in distaste. "I'm from Miami," he went on to inform them, "I'm a writer, and I'm thinking about doing a novel set in Norway."

Carla was fascinated, and said she had never met a real writer before. Jenny asked what he'd had published, and he admitted he was more or less on sabbatical from his regular job as an office equipment salesman and was determined to "find himself," which, translated, meant to her he had never written anything, thus reinforcing her opinion he was a phony.

At last, Carla held up the card. "Athena."

"Wonderful. So am I. Let's go see if we can all get a table together."

"Oh, great!" Carla turned to Jenny. "Isn't this neat? Now we've got a threesome."

Jenny felt a flash of regret that Carla was falling so easily but had no intention of getting involved in her affairs. Linda's deceit had made her extremely leery of ever having a close girlfriend again. "You two go ahead," she said. "I'll take the jackets back to the cabin."

Already they were on their way, forgetting all about her.

Jenny went inside, but, in her haste and weariness from her long journey, took a wrong turn. Her ship's guide book was back in the cabin, and she tried to remember, Was it *blue* carpet that led *forward,* or *aft?* And was her cabin *starboard* or *port side?* Oh, dear Lord, she was so tired, and it seemed the more she walked, the more confused she became. She knew she was on the right deck, but the ship was enormous, and it was easy to get turned around, especially in her exhausted state.

She reached an elevator bank, and there was a sofa in the hallway, and suddenly she felt the need to rest a little before stumbling on. She sat down to get her bearings.

"May I be of assistance?"

Jenny looked up to find herself drowning once more in Kirk Moen's devastatingly blue eyes, and could not find her voice.

Kirk was watching her mouth, wondering what it would be like to kiss her. He wanted to reach down then and there and pull her into his arms, and— *Stop it!* he commanded. Just another cruise. *No way!* Why torture himself? He made his voice stern. "Are you lost, Miss Denton?"

Suddenly she felt very foolish and quickly stood. "No," she lied, embarrassed. "I'm just resting."

A smile touched his lips, but he maintained his cool demeanor of authority. "I recall you're in the Venus suite. Just follow the blue stars in the silver carpet, then red on gold, and you'll find it."

He gave her a mock salute, turned, walked away—but reluctantly.

Jenny could not resist turning to watch as he made his way down the hall to wherever he was going, and she smiled as she did so.

There was just something about a man in a uniform!

And this one had terrific buns!

FOUR

"You can wear that tonight, if you like," Jenny said when Carla returned to the suite.

Carla's eyes grew wide with pleasure as she held up the soft pink sweater and the white cotton slacks. "Are you sure it's all right for me to wear these?" she gasped. "I mean, they're beautiful!"

"Sure. They'll look great with your coloring. And I think they'll fit. The slacks are a size eight and the sweater a small."

"That's me." Carla headed for the shower. "I'm just glad tonight's dress is casual for dinner. Tomorrow night is formal, though. I just hope my luggage catches up with me in Bergen."

Jenny had already thought of that and decided she would lend her a cocktail dress.

When they were ready, they headed for the dining room. "I'm glad we've got second seating," Carla remarked. "I heard it's better because nobody rushes you to get out so they can get ready for the next feeding of the herd."

"Gives us longer when we're in port, too," Jenny pointed out.

They reached the entrance to the Athena dining room, where steps from left and right met at a small landing before the final descent. A young man with a Jamaican accent, dressed in short white coat and shiny black trousers, was waiting at the bottom of the stairway to ask what table number they had been assigned. Carla produced a card at precisely the same moment that Russ appeared, in fresh shirt, tie, jacket, and dark trousers. "I'll take them," he said to the waiter, as he held out his hand to Carla.

Jenny followed along, pleased that they had managed to get a table by one of the large windows looking out on the sea. It was already dark out, but the view, she knew, would be splendid by day.

A young man with a dark complexion and warm brown eyes appeared tableside to cheerfully announce, "Welcome. I am Miguel, your waiter."

Jenny looked at the folder she had been given and winced at the thought of what her scale would read if she indulged in such treats for fourteen days. Seven kinds of appetizers, from fruit cups to pizza. Three kinds of soups and four varieties of salads, six entrées, covering everything that swam, crawled, flew, or just ambled along. At the sight of the dessert list, she squeezed her eyes closed and refused to look any further. She ordered vichyssoise and a crab salad and handed the menu back to Miguel.

"Who is to sit there?" Jenny indicated the empty seat.

"We are missing one passenger who failed to make his flight connections," Miguel was quick to explain. "He will join us in our first port—Bergen." He hurried away to fill their orders.

Jenny enjoyed her food but found herself feeling very, very alone. All around her people seemed to be with someone—couples, families, groups traveling together. At her own table, she felt left out of everything, because Russ was bent on charming Carla, who was obligingly hanging on to his every word. Finally, after a dangerously delicious dessert of chocolate mousse smothered in whipped cream, Jenny decided she'd had enough of feeling like an outsider. "I'm going to call it a day," she said to Carla as she prepared to leave. "I'm really tired."

"No!" Carla protested. "This is our first night on board. You can't go to bed like an old fuddy-duddy. Come with us."

It did not take much persuasion. Jenny had not come on the cruise to pine away, alone in her cabin, while everyone else was out having fun. Besides, she needed to mingle, to move around and familiarize herself with the ship and all it had to offer so she could better organize her presentation to Valhalla's CEO's when the time came. Just after returning from the lifeboat drill, a message from the radio operator informed her that she had received an invitation to a party in Oslo hosted by the line's executives. That would be in the last week of the cruise, and she wanted something to offer by then.

"Okay," she said finally. "If I won't be in the way . . ."

"Nonsense," Carla assured. "The more the merrier, right, Russ?" She looked up at him adoringly.

Jenny took note of the slight frown that touched his brow and the way a shadow of displeasure crossed his face.

With a stiff smile, he coolly said, "I think I'd like to try my luck in the casino."

"Later!" Carla promised. "Right now, let's go, so we can get a good seat."

Jenny thought the show was fun, with singers and dancers and a stand-up comic. He reminded her of Billy Crystal and that made her laugh till her sides hurt. When it was over, and the waiter brought the check to be signed, Jenny took note that Russ had chosen that precise time to excuse himself. The tab was less than twenty dollars, and she moved to sign it, but Carla jerked it away and said, "No, no, I'll get it. I have some money right here—"

"We don't take cash," the waiter was quick to inform her.

Carla looked at Jenny, bewildered. "What's he talking about? *They don't take money?*"

"You have to register a credit card at the purser's office," Jenny explained. "Then, on the last day of the cruise, you go by, collect your tickets, settle up, and sign the charge slip."

"Well, I've got a credit card."

Jenny shook her head. "You can't use it now. He can't take it. Go to the purser's office tomorrow morning. I'll get this. I stopped by after the lifeboat drill and registered my card."

"Well. . . ." Carla said uncertainly. "I'll pay you back later."

"Don't worry about it," Jenny emphasized.

Russ returned just as the waiter was walking away with the check and he pretended to be embarrassed. "I was going to get that. Why didn't you just tell him I'd be back in a minute?"

Jenny thought he was real good. She had to hand him that. He almost sounded convincing, knew that if he was, he'd have gone after the waiter instead of just watching him disappear out of sight. Not that she minded picking up the tab; she wouldn't have let him pay for her drinks anyway. It was just so disgusting that he was such a con artist.

"So!" Russ suddenly grinned, rubbed his hands together in a gesture of anticipation. "Let's hit the casino. I feel lucky."

"Are you coming with us, Jenny?" Carla was quick to ask.

She shook her head. "You two have fun," she said, hurrying out before Carla could try to dissuade her.

Jenny wandered around the ship, not knowing what to do with herself, knowing only that she hated to do nothing but go to bed. Everywhere she looked, she was painfully reminded of how alone she was. This was the first time in her life she had traveled without a companion, and she was finding out it was not a lot of fun. But it was early, and she decided maybe she should go back and write in her journal awhile, then go to the disco later.

On her way back to the suite, she decided to step outside to view the ocean at night. The wind was brisk and cold as she moved to stand at the railing. Her meticulously coiffed hair was soon blowing wildly about her face, and she could feel the salty sting of the ocean spray against her cheeks. Yet she did not move. A full moon sprinkled the black ocean with diamonds, and she could imagine fairies dancing in the silver foam that laced the huge, dark waves.

Suddenly she realized she had *never* felt so lonely. Oh, it was so easy to see why people did have whirlwind shipboard romances, for it was a temporary journey into fantasy, where dreams could come true—if only for the duration of the cruise.

With a shiver in the chilly night air, she was about to turn and go inside but hesitated as she saw the lights of a ship on the horizon, far, far away. It reminded her of a poem she had once loved. She tried to recall the words, began to murmur out loud as she gripped the railing and gazed toward the light. "Ships . . . that pass in the night . . ." *But what was the next line?* Suddenly it seemed so important, a needed balm.

From the shadows, Kirk had been silently watching her

and wondering whether he should make his presence known. Ever since the drill, and their later meeting at the elevator, he could not get her image out of his mind. Maybe she was different from the rest and not the type just to live out a fantasy, not caring whose heart she broke in the process. It might not even make any difference if she knew who he really was.

Taking a deep breath, he stepped forward to recite softly the rest of the poem she was trying to remember. "Ships that pass in the night, and speak to each other in passing, only a signal shown and a distant voice in the darkness. So on the ocean of life we pass and speak to one another, only a look and a voice, then darkness again and a silence."

She stared in wonder.

It was *him*.

He smiled in the moonlight, "It's from Longfellow's 'Elizabeth, IV.' "

"Thank you." She managed to find her voice, and stammered, "It . . . it seemed apropos, somehow."

"A beautiful poem but with a sad connotation. People shouldn't pass like ships in the night. They should take time to get to know each other." He moved to stand beside her at the railing.

Jenny did not know what to say, because his nearness was so disconcerting.

"I understand you are the young lady who wants the Valhalla contract for Publicity and Promotion."

She quickly turned to stare up at him. "That's right. Word travels fast."

"I was told you were coming on board, and I was planning to call you tomorrow and offer my assistance."

"That's wonderful. I can use a guided tour. This boat is so big."

He laughed and gently chided, "The *Misty Seas* is a

ship, Miss Denton. Not a *boat*. Remember, you can put a boat on a ship, but not a ship on a boat.''

''Aye, aye, sir!'' She gave him the same kind of mock salute he'd given her at the elevator, clicked her heels together, and assured him that she stood corrected. The humor, she hoped, helped to camouflage the maelstrom of emotions churning within her.

Suddenly, the wind seemed to pick up, and Jenny actually staggered a step backward from its vicious assault. Kirk caught her arm, was quick to suggest, ''I think we'd better get inside now. I was reading a weather bulletin in the radio room a little while ago that said to expect squalls tonight.''

His hand closed about her arm as they moved to the heavy doors leading back inside the ship. Jenny felt a warm rush at his possessive touch, and regretted his release seconds later.

They were standing in a small lobby between the entrance to a bar on one side and a nightclub on the other. They found themselves surrounded by people moving about, but, as their gazes met and held, it was as though no one else existed in the whole world.

Kirk wanted to kiss her. Then and there. And never had he wanted to feel a woman in his arms more. It was times like this he hated adhering to the code of being an officer *and* a gentleman. Maybe the blood of his Viking ancestors was boiling, because he would have liked to lift her up and carry her off to his cabin . . . make wild, passionate love to her all night long. Just thinking about what it would be like to caress her smooth, warm, naked body was making him start to feel extremely uncomfortable in his tight trousers. He knew if he didn't soon muster some self-control, he was going to be embarrassed. He decided to make conversation fast, get his mind on something else. ''So, start thinking how I can help, and I'll give you a call tomorrow after we leave Bergen. We can set a time to meet.''

Jenny was drowning again, felt absolutely feverish, wondered if the heat within was making her face flush, because her cheeks felt terribly hot. ''That . . . that would be nice,'' she managed to say. ''I'd like that.'' All the while she was thinking how she did not want this moment to end. All around her people were having fun, and she wanted to be like them, did not want to relegate herself to isolation and misery. No matter that she was still not quite over the breakup with Bryan. That was then. This was *now*. And this gorgeous, blond-haired, blue-eyed hunk with the sexy accent had her absolutely on fire. Somehow she knew he was feeling the same desire for her. Even in the early days of the-wonder-of-me-and-you with Bryan she had never felt this way. Kirk Moen had not even kissed her, *yet,* and already she could feel the moisture of her body's desire at just his nearness. *What madness was this?*

Kirk's eyes were locked with hers once more, and he could sense what she was feeling. It was as though their bodies had tuned in to each other like computer hookups. Conversation, he knew, was not going to replace a cold shower, and he needed to get out of there fast. Hoping his nervousness did not show, he repeated, ''I'll call you tomorrow afternoon.''

Jenny was still reluctant for him to go. ''Are you going ashore tomorrow?''

He nodded, devouring her with his gaze, his fingers twitching ever so slightly with the overwhelming desire to reach out and grab her and hold her close against his body so she could feel the hardness of his desire. ''Yes,'' he murmured in a strained voice he did not recognize as his own. ''It's my home port. I get to see my family, do a few things around the house.''

She felt a painful jolt in her heart, could not help blurting out, "You're married?"

"No," he laughed, grateful for the chance to lighten the tension that hung over them like an invisible shroud. "I own a house there. My mother lives in it. I've also got an aunt and an uncle in Bergen."

Finally, in almost a whisper, he offered, "There's a lecture on Norwegian folklore in the *Viking Queen* ballroom tomorrow evening, right after we leave Bergen. I think you might enjoy it. Would you meet me there?"

"I'd love to," Jenny said without hesitation.

"Good. I'll see you around five-thirty."

She turned toward the elevator rather than the stairway. Though her suite was only two decks above, she did not trust her suddenly trembling legs to carry her along with any grace, especially with him staring after her.

Then, just as the elevator doors opened, Kirk impulsively stepped in with her. "I'll ride with you to your deck."

The elevator began to move. They continued to look at each other, sending secret messages of passionate desire. Suddenly, Kirk reached out and pushed the Stop button, bringing them to a jolting halt. From somewhere in the distance came the sound of the emergency bell ringing, but neither Kirk nor Jenny heard, for they were listening only to their bodies, their hearts. With one quick movement, he pulled her against him, brought his lips crashing down on hers. Jenny stood on tiptoe, straining to get ever closer, parting her lips for the delicious taste of his probing tongue. She could feel his hardness against her, as she felt her own moisture increasing. Dear God, where would the madness lead? her tormented brain screamed.

He released her to stare down at her in feverish challenge. "I have a bottle of wine in my cabin."

Tremulously, she whispered, "I have champagne on ice in mine."

"Officers aren't allowed in female passengers' cabins." He trailed a fingertip gently, lovingly, down her cheek.

She trembled at his touch. "Why not?"

His smile was absolutely wicked. "They might scream rape."

"And what's to prevent a woman from screaming that in *your* cabin?" she countered saucily.

He winked. "She goes of her own free will. She takes her chances the officer might make a pass."

"Aren't you making one now?"

"No." He kissed the tip of her nose, slipped his arm around her waist to pull her close, and claim her mouth again before assuring her that she'd know it when he did, "So, care to take a chance?" he challenged.

Jenny drew away from his embrace, put her hands on her hips, tilted her head to one side, and, in her best Bette Davis imitation cracked, "I say, fasten your seat belts. It's gonna be a bumpy ride!"

He touched another button, sending the elevator into motion once more and reaching for her at the same time.

He took her beyond the forbidding door with its Officers Only sign, and they quietly made their way down the gray-carpeted hallway. They passed closed doors on each side, and Jenny had a fleeting glimpse of little metal strips in holders beside each, with Norwegian names and denoting their ranks. There was no sound except the faint, gentle swish of the turbines from far below in the bowels of the great ship.

He stopped outside a door with a strip identifying: MOEN, K.—CHIEF OFFICER SENIOR. He took a key from his pocket, unlocked the door, opened it, then stepped back for her to enter.

Inside, she glanced around to see that he also had a suite. Not as large or luxurious as hers, but the main room was furnished with a sofa, chair, and coffee table. There was a TV set and a VCR on a shelf opposite. Down a short hallway, she could see a desk and bookshelves along one wall and what looked like a wet bar on the other side, with shelves above it. A closed curtain barred further view into sleeping quarters.

Kirk touched a wall switch, and they were at once surrounded by the romantic music of Richard Clayderman. Yet another switch mellowed the lights.

The tension between them was almost smothering in its intensity. Every time he looked at her, she felt a tremor within. Her palms felt moist, sweaty. Never, ever had a man affected her this way.

He went to the wet bar, took out a bottle of Moselle. "Is this all right?" he asked.

"Fine. Fine." She sat down on the sofa, watched as he opened the wine and filled two glasses.

He sat down beside her, and she took a big sip of the cold wine, and, relishing the sudden mellow wave within, quickly took another.

He had set the bottle down on the coffee table and moved to refill her glass as he murmured, "This is much nicer than being in one of the lounges at this hour. They're all crowded. Noisy."

"You have a nice cabin."

"Well, I live here, you know, and I find it kind of cramped at times. Fortunately I'm not here much. Just to sleep. Take a shower."

Jenny said she understood. He asked whether she liked her suite. Small talk. Meaningless. Meant only to mask the awareness that had every nerve in both their bodies silently screaming.

Jenny wondered whether it was happening too fast, if she should just finish her wine, leave, sleep on her emotions, and decide whether she really wanted to get involved before she did.

But that was not what she wanted to do.

She *did* want to get involved.

She already was.

He kept refilling her glass and she kept sipping, feeling

more and more relaxed. Gradually, the turmoil within her was quelled.

At last the bottle was empty. Somewhere along the way they were in each other's arms, kissing 'til they were breathless . . . kisses like warm, sweet wine.

His hand slipped beneath her sweater, then her bra, to gently knead her breasts as though testing succulent fruit for ripeness. Wanting more, he reached to unfasten the bra, and she moved to help him, then drew her sweater up and over her head, offering herself to him freely as she turned sideways to lie back on the sofa. With thumb and forefinger, he lightly pinched each nipple in turn to hardness. The tips of their tongues were hungrily teasing, then greedily devouring.

He moved to trail dancing fingers across her belly, at the same time his lips moved from hers to trace down her neck. She gasped in anticipation as he ignited fire across her chest, finally touching a nipple with a tormenting flick of his tongue. Around, around, ever so lightly, then almost roughly sucking in as much as he could within his mouth, again and again.

Jenny felt as though she were about to explode, could not be still, her own hands moving up and down his back to clutch in eager desperation. She could feel his hardness against her, dizzily thought how huge he was going to be, *wanting* him inside her. She began to undulate her hips beneath him, and he paused in his feasting of her breasts to raggedly warn, "Oh, my darling, don't do that . . . not yet . . ."

"Now . . ." she begged. "I need you now . . ."

He paused to smile down at her. "Never have dessert first. Enjoy each course."

Boldly, she moved to touch him *there*, dizzily wondering how his trousers held together against the massive trobbing. "Dessert. *Now*," she boldly commanded.

Never, she realized in wonder, had she been so brazen, feeling no inhibitions whatsoever. "I want you now . . ."

He got up then, to lift her quickly in his arms and carry her through the curtained partition to the bedroom. A lamp on the table bathed them in a mellow light. He did not lay her down on the bed, instead, he set her on her feet to stand before him. He held her away from him, cupping and squeezing her breasts, once more massaging her nipples between his fingertips. "I want to undress you," he whispered huskily. "I've wanted to see you naked from the first moment I laid eyes on you at the drill. All I could think about was wondering how you'd look naked, knew you'd be exquisite . . ."

Jenny swayed with wonder and the desire that consumed like molten lava through her veins.

He unfastened her skirt. She stepped out of it as though hypnotized, like a bird held in a trance before a snake's mesmerizing glare. Only Kirk's eyes were anything but malevolent. The expression she saw there was one of lust, hot and savage.

He tormented himself with the delicious feeling of running his hands up and down her firm thighs, reaching to grasp her high rounded buttocks. Never, in all his years of manhood, could Kirk remember wanting a woman more. And, despite his gnawing passion, the torture of holding back, he knew, somehow, there was more behind all that he was feeling. Jenny Denton possessed a mystical, magical quality that had never been present in any of his past relationships. He knew he wanted her, had to have her, just as he knew he wanted more than a meeting of the flesh. He wanted a melding of the mind, a meeting of heart and spirit. But those wondrous experiences would have to come later. For the moment, the pleasures of the flesh had to be answered or he was going to explode, then and there.

He hooked his thumbs in her panty hose, drawing them down as she yielded.

Then she was naked before him.

"My turn," she tremulously declared, reaching to loosen his tie as he hurriedly yanked off his white coat. Flinging the tie aside, she nimbly worked at the buttons. At last his broad, muscular chest was revealed, the mat of curling sand-blond hair tapering on down a taut stomach to disappear beneath the waist of the trousers she struggled to unfasten. Because of his heated desire, she could not release the zipper, and he laughed softly as he moved to assist her.

Jenny could not hold back the gasp of awe as he was rendered into her waiting hands. At first she was hesitant, then, as he stepped out of his garments, her fingertips became braver, exploring his erection. They danced downward, to cup and fondle all of him. In turn, he slipped his hand between her legs, felt her moisture, was confident her fervor nearly equaled his own.

He lowered her to the bed, stretched out beside her, showering her face with kisses as he manipulated to caress the nucleus of her womanhood, feeling it swell beneath his massaging fingers.

Jenny did not recognize her voice as her own, pleading, an almost-whimper. "Please . . . please take me now . . ."

But Kirk wanted the magic to last, wanted to ensure that when the final moment of ecstasy came, the pinnacle of all their sensory emotions, that they would ultimately travel to that glorious peak together.

He lowered his mouth to again suckle her breast at the exact moment she reached for him once more, and he knew he had reached his own point of surrender. He moved on top of her, and she eagerly raised her legs to wrap about him, heels tucked upon his buttocks. He began to kiss her again, and it was as though she could not get enough of his lips, his tongue, and her nails dug into the rock-hard flesh of his back, wanting him yet closer, clinging to him.

He began his entry, and Jenny tensed. Wildly, wickedly, she had giggled in earlier years with girlfriends over the size of men's sexual organs, only in jest, in fun, never in serious pondering. Now, though, she knew this was her own, special, wonderful secret as he filled her with his hugeness.

She came at once.

The explosion started from deep within and spread through her belly and into her loins, taking her by surprise, and she cried out and dug her nails in yet harder as his movements quickened, became almost rough in stride. He could feel her climax, yet did not slow, and Jenny continued to devour his mouth between ragged gasps. She could not believe it was not yet over, that the sensory edge was still raw, eager, hungry for more. Somehow she knew it would happen again, a never-before experience, one that would forever be remembered as the moment she knew what it truly meant to be a woman . . . in the loving arms of a man.

Kirk marveled at her response. Never had he had such a tigress. Never had he felt such emotion in a woman. And, even in the throes of his own impending release, he knew, somehow, that his life, his heart, had changed forever. Never would he forget Jenny Denton. Never would he allow her to forget *him*. This was not merely sex, desire, lust, coupling . . . whatever name it might be called. This was the beginning of *love,* deep and strong and pure, for such an awesome encounter could be inspired by nothing less.

With every shred of self-control he could muster, Kirk held back until his senses told him Jenny was ready once more, and only then did he allow himself blessed relief from the torturous hunger of his loins.

She cried out loud, in wonder, in awe, in rapture, as they crested together, riding to the highest cloud of joy to quiver and tremble in the immensity of the moment.

Slowly, at last, with Kirk's movements becoming gentle, they transcended to earth and reality once more. They rolled to one side, arms and legs still entwined, sealing the wonder of it all with a last, lingering kiss.

Jenny slept peacefully, and Kirk watched her in complete adoration. So beautiful. So precious. Crazy though it might be, he knew he was falling in love with her. There had to be time, however, before he could let her know that, lest history repeat itself. He thought of the women before her that he had dared to get too involved with. So many times they came on board, looking for fun, romance. So many times he had been left feeling like a fool. He recalled the one who had lied about not being married—Brenda. Why had she bothered to string him along, giving him her phone number in Memphis? The first Saturday the ship returned to Miami after she'd left, he called her, only to hear a man's voice growl that he was Brenda's husband, and ask what the hell Kirk wanted.

Brenda was only one of many who had lied, rather than admit they were only out for a good time, a shipboard romance as part of their vacation memoirs.

He thought of other encounters, like the ones who found out he was heir to much stock in Valhalla Lines, that he was actually the nephew of one of the CEO's. He was on the ship to learn everything there was to know, and he worked hard, by God. He wasn't merely biding his time until he received his inheritance. But some of the other crew members, no doubt jealous, liked to gossip, and when some women found out he'd be rich one day, they started hearing wedding bells. He was sick of them. He wanted, needed, a real and honest woman who cared only for him, not what he was. One day he wanted to marry again. Glenna had been a youthful mistake that did not work out, but he accepted that failed union for what it was and would not let it shadow a future attempt for marital bliss.

He brushed back a wisp of Jenny's strawberry-blond hair and kissed her forehead lovingly. For the past year he had kept a tight rein on his heart. There had been women, of course. He was a man, with a man's needs, and had to admit that the ambience of a cruise ship was conducive to romance. Yet he had promised no woman anything, had given a few a good time on their cruise, made sure they were satisfied sexually. Then there was a kiss good-bye in port, and if they wrote to him, he replied. A few returned for later cruises. He had learned to steer clear of those who wanted more than a casual fling, for he did not want to hurt anyone and wanted to spare himself any more heartache. As a result, he had many, many close friendships with women who only wanted a good time. And that suited him just fine.

But you, little girl, he whispered as he got out of bed and tucked the Norwegian down comforter about Jenny, *are special.* She did not know it yet, but she had already stolen his heart, and he intended to do everything in his power to steal hers, as well.

A glance at the clock on the bedside table told him it was well after midnight, and he had promised the night watch officer to take his post, in exchange for being able to relinquish his duties for a day's leave in Bergen.

He quickly showered and changed into a fresh white uniform. Hastily, he scribbled a note to Jenny telling her he would be very pleased if she would accompany him ashore. He wanted her to meet his family. Take her to lunch. Show her the sights. He propped the note beside the phone so she would see it when he phoned her just before six o'clock, when they would be entering the Bergen fjord.

He brushed his lips across hers, smiled as she sleepily stirred, then left.

SIX

Jenny awoke with a start, and wondered for an instant where she was. Then it all came flooding back—the wonder of it all.

She lay there, basking in the warm afterglow, then reached out to touch Kirk's pillow, wishing he were still there with her but knowing he must have had to report for duty.

With a contented sigh, she sat up to push the curtain above the bed aside and stare out at the night, but it wasn't dark. The world was tinted in the strange peach hue of the midnight sun, and she thought it all so beautiful—as beautiful as the hours in Kirk's arms.

Now it seemed like a dream, but she could revel in the knowledge it had all been quite real. And, she told herself with a smile as she flung back the covers to clamber out of bed, it all went to prove that life isn't over because some men can be creeps!

She did not notice that the comforter had brushed the bedside table, sending Kirk's note fluttering to the floor.

She dressed quickly. A glance at her watch told her it

was nearly five A.M. She wanted to get back to her own cabin, shower, and get out on deck for her first glimpse of landfall in Norway.

Now, she thought, if she could only remember how to find her way out of there and back into the passenger section. Opening the door, she peered into the hallway, grateful to find it empty, then quickly made her way out, breathing a sigh of relief each time she chose the right turn, the right door.

When she reached her suite, she was not surprised to find Carla's bed empty. It had been pretty obvious the night before that she was very smitten with Russ Claiborne. Jenny only hoped she wasn't in for a big heartache, but reminded herself not to get involved. She had enough problems of her own to deal with, without getting involved with the problems of another girlfriend.

She showered, changed, and was getting ready to go up on deck when Carla came in. "Hi," she greeted cheerily, sleepily. "I figured I'd have to wake you up, but I see you're an early bird."

"We're coming into port, and I thought I'd go up on deck and take some pictures."

Carla went to the window and looked out, marveling, "They call it the Land of the Midnight Sun, because during the summer months, it's never really night. Russ and I went out on deck around three this morning, after the casino closed, and it wasn't even dark then. It's like someone threw a big blanket over all the lights in the whole world. It was eerie."

"If you stayed in the casino that late, Russ must've been right about saying he felt lucky," Jenny could not help remarking.

She frowned. "Not really. He lost a little, but he says it's no big deal. He'll win it back tonight. Said he just had to get the feel of the tables."

Jenny went on to shower and was just drying off when the phone rang. Her heart leaped! Though she had no idea when Kirk had left during the night, she figured he had returned, found her gone, and was now calling. She waited, held her breath, hoping Carla would say it was for her.

A moment later Carla squealed loudly, "That's great. Terrific! I can't believe it. Oh, thanks so much for letting me know." She hung up the phone and yelled to Jenny through the door, "That was the radio operator. He says the cruise line office in Bergen just notified they have my luggage. It will be delivered to the ship today."

Jenny sighed with her own disappointment but called back to agree that was wonderful news. "Want to go up on deck with me?" she asked, coming out of the bathroom.

"Shower first," Carla said, heading for her turn.

Jenny was wearing slacks, a cotton sweater, a light jacket, and Reeboks for the walking she intended to do in Bergen. She had received a package from Valhalla describing all the land tours available but decided to forgo anything organized for this port, wanting instead to go on her own. She could not help thinking of how it was Kirk's hometown, how nice it would have been if they could go ashore together and he could show her around.

As she waited for Carla to get ready, she stood at the window and stared out pensively at the shoreline of the Bergen fjord. She could see sparse houses, a few buildings perched up on cliffs that appeared to be bunkers left over from World War II.

Gradually, like a silent, creeping spider among the cobwebs of her brain, she was carried back in time, contemplating once more where she had gone wrong in her personal life.

Before they actually met, Jenny was well aware of who

Bryan was. He drove a bright red Porsche through Atlanta traffic weekdays, while weekends found him either sailing the waters of Lake Hartwell in his boat or riding Morgan horses on his parents' magnificent farm near Covington. He was a patron of the arts and no stranger to the society pages of the Atlanta *Constitution*, usually pictured with a dewy-eyed debutante clinging to his arm. He was, without a doubt, considered one of the most eligible bachelors in the South and had once even been featured as such in *Town and Country* magazine.

Jenny, however, had her own wealth of self-confidence and never stood in awe of Bryan Morrow from the moment they met—which had been a rather inauspicious situation. An elderly woman had dropped dead in one of the Zippy Pizza stores after consuming a cheese-and-anchovy concoction. Her family, poor and illiterate, had been pounced upon by an ambulance-chasing lawyer before the deceased was even in the ground. He convinced them they had a good suit against Zippy, sure that the CEO's would gladly settle with the bereaved out of court rather than suffer the consequences of a much-publicized court trial. Zippy hired Bryan's firm, and Bryan was assigned the case. He refused a settlement and let the pompous lawyer for the plaintiffs take the case to court. Subsequently he made the plaintiff look like a fool by presenting medical records that the woman had a history of heart problems, was supposed to be on a strict, low-fat diet, and rich, spicy foods were forbidden. With an autopsy report disclosing cause of death as heart failure, the jury yielded to Bryan's charm and methodical presentation of facts and determined that the deceased would have expired at that point in time, no matter *where* she was or *what* she had just eaten.

Jenny, in her role of account supervisor for Zippy, had been present throughout the short trial. She had, of course, been formally introduced to Bryan, but there had been no eye contact or flirting, no reason at all to think he was interested in her other than professionally. But when the judge banged the gavel and declared court was adjourned, Bryan had turned to her and suggested with a warm smile, "How about celebrating over steaks and a bottle of Cristal?"

That had been the beginning of a whirlwind romance that swept Jenny off her feet to the tune of every poignant love song ever written and recorded. In less than a month, she was leaving her clothes in a closet in his penthouse in the heart of Atlanta so she would not have to travel back and forth during the week to her townhouse. Weekends they were on his boat or at his parents' farm. In yet another month, Jenny left her townhouse to the care of *then* best friend, Linda and moved in with Bryan. Their friends and associates were delighted and regarded Jenny and Bryan as a *Camelot* couple, destined to be together.

And that was what Jenny thought, too . . . for over a year. They were inseparable, or so she believed. There was the fall cruise to Mexico, and then they had spent Thanksgiving with her parents. Christmas they enjoyed with Bryan's family on holiday in their lavish Hilton Head retreat. He gave her an expensive diamond tennis bracelet. For a New Year's vacation they jetted to Aspen amidst movie stars and TV celebrities. At Easter, they took a cruise to Cozumel, and that was when she found the huge engagement ring sparkling up at her from a glass of champagne.

They looked at crystal and china. They talked of the house they would build on the velvet hillock that overlooked the splendid farm that one day Bryan would inherit. They even talked of the children they wanted someday, though Bryan understood her need, her drive, for a career of her own. And they began to think about a wedding date, wanting to plan a time around Jenny's travels to her clients' stores and Bryan's court docket. A honeymoon cruise on the *QE-II* was also discussed.

Through it all, Jenny never questioned her feelings for Bryan. Everything was so perfect. She accepted, without doubt, that they were truly meant to be together and foresaw no problems. Her only concern in life was the increasing ennui with her job, and she became obsessed with finding a solution.

Well, she reflected with a sigh of resignation, it would seem that her major career move had resulted in the breakup with Bryan. But it was not totally fair to say that, either. Bryan's kind, unfortunately, could probably never be faithful to just one woman. And that was something Jenny truly believed in—unwavering loyalty when two people were committed to each other. Never, in any past relationship with a man, had she ever been deceitful. Each romance had died a natural death, with or without regrets, but not one time had she ever felt betrayed. *Till Bryan.* So she was better off, she knew, and, one day, it would not hurt so bad when that spider of the past momentarily held her fast in the web of painful memories.

Carla came out, wrapped in a towel, a hesitant smile on her face. "Could you lend me something just for today, just till I get my suitcase? I mean, I *slept* in your clothes last night, and—"

"Sure," Jenny cut her off, not wanting to dwell on the situation, because she doubted Carla had slept with clothes on any more than she had. She went to the closet, took out a fresh pair of slacks and another sweater. "Sorry I don't have a spare jacket, but I've got a raincoat."

"Sure. That would be fine."

Jenny looked at the crumpled clothes that she had lent her the night before lying on the bed. Would Carla think to send them to the ship's laundry? She doubted it, and went to the desk and took out a plastic bag, tags, and saw to it herself.

Carla, busy rolling her hair on borrowed hot rollers, was oblivious to anything so mundane. "I really like Russ," she suddenly confided. "He's quite a guy. Fascinating. Just think. He's going to write a book on Norway. He quit his job to take off and do research. That took a lot of guts, you know? I mean, how many people would have the courage to do that?"

As Carla raved on, singing the praises of Russ Claiborne, Jenny tuned her out as she continued to stare out the window, lost in her own pleasant ponderings. Kirk was quite a man, all right. And no longer than she'd known him, she could tell he was quite intelligent, of good background, charming, witty—everything a woman could want.

"What did you do last night?" Carla suddenly wanted to know, curious as to why Jenny was staring out the window like her mind was a million miles away.

"I went to bed," Jenny said curtly, not meaning to sound so abrupt but not wanting to confide anything, either. Another lesson learned. She had shared too many secrets with Linda. Secrets, which, after what had happened, Linda would probably not hold sacred any longer. *Never again!* "Are you ready?" she prodded.

"Sure," Carla happily responded. "Maybe I'll even get to wave at my suitcases when they come on board. I'll be so glad to see them!"

From the top deck, they could see everything and noted other passengers shared their enthusiasm over the first glimpse of Norway, as the railings were quite crowded.

The wind was cold, and Carla quickly changed her mind and went back inside. Jenny pulled out the scarf she had stuffed into her pocket to tie around her hair. Then, cameras ready, the light meters adjusted to the delicate milky light, she focused on the shoreline which was just starting to come into view.

From the gray North Sea, the rocks and islets and skerries of a grim coast drifted swiftly by as they headed inland, up a deep slice of saltwater, knifing toward the towering mountains.

She turned to look below her, to the flying bridge, the extension of the inner navigational area. Several officers stood there. They were wearing dress uniforms and hats and made an impressive sight. She looked for Kirk but did not see him with the others, and decided he must be below in the engine room. Then, suddenly, he stepped outside, and she felt the familiar thrilling rush as he turned his head at once to look upward, scanning the crowd, his eyes falling on her. He grinned, saluted, and she happily waved back.

Finally, he disappeared inside, and she forced her attention to the moment at hand. Consulting her guide book, she knew they were sailing into Holsnfjord, which lay at the foot of what was called Mount Fløyen. And, at last, the city of Bergen came into view with its famed gingerbread villages. Graduating elevations of houses with red-tiled roofs seemed to stand as sentinels over the harbor from which the dreaded Norsemen set out on their raids over nine hundred years ago. She was eager to learn everything she could about the country and its history, for she felt Valhalla was not using the Norwegian culture to its advantage.

As soon as the ship began to approach the dock, Jenny hurried to the dining room.

The aroma in the dining room was tantalizing with the delicious smells of bacon and eggs and fresh pastry right out of the oven. Jenny saw that Carla and Russ were already seated, but there was also a strange face at the table—a very nice and friendly face, she was quick to note.

He stood, smiling warmly and eagerly. "Hi, I'm Steve Gentry. I flew in with Carla's luggage."

Jenny sat down beside him in the chair he obligingly held out for her. "So you're the one who missed the boat . . . uh, *ship,*" she quickly corrected with a private smile, "in Amsterdam." He had to be thirty-something, late thirty-something with slight graying at the temples of his thick black hair. He had coffee-colored eyes, a Roman nose, pencil-thin mustache, and a Kirk Douglas cleft in his chin. He sported a deep tan, evident of someone who stays outdoors a lot. Probably athletic, judging from what she could see of his body tone in the tight designer jeans and form-fitting Alexander Julian shirt.

He waited till she had given Miguel her breakfast order—poached egg on English muffin, tomato juice, coffee—then said, "Carla tells me you're from Atlanta. So am I."

She was pleasantly surprised. "Really, what part?"

"My office is on the west side, but I have an apartment on the east side. How about you?"

"I have a townhouse near Decatur."

"And your office?"

She thought a moment, then looked at him in wonder as she remembered that, for the time being, she really didn't *have* an office. She had been so busy getting ready for the cruise, working out her notice with Cuisine Unlimited, that there hadn't been time to think about renting space, hiring an assistant, any of the many requirements for starting her own business. "I don't have one," she admitted.

"Oh?" He raised an eyebrow. He glanced at Carla. "But she was telling me you're in public relations . . . advertising."

"I am. I'm just in the process of starting my own business and haven't rented office space yet."

"Well, what agency were you with before?"

She told him, and suddenly he snapped his fingers and grinned. "Now I know who you are. The name didn't ring a bell, but you're the genius who came up with the idea of Astro Cookies. And I heard Cuisine Unlimited was really upset when you gave notice you were going out on your own. I know, because I'm an architect, and I'm working on two malls right now, and both already have reservations for cookie shacks, primarily to sell *your* Astro Cookies."

"Gee, Jenny, that's great," Carla said, impressed.

Jenny attempted to shrug off Steve's praise. "Well, the cookies are tasteless," she said. "I mean, people are just willing to spend a dollar to read their horoscope."

"But no one thought of that except *you*," he was quick to point out, "and it turned out to be one hell of a gimmick. People were starting to get tired of paying almost a dollar a piece for a chocolate-chip cookie, and I designed three malls last year that didn't have *one* single cookie corner. The popularity was down, and you've built them back up. Astro franchises are making a fortune, thanks to you."

Carla again interjected. "I didn't know all this about you, Jenny. Gosh. That's great."

"And now you're branching out on your own." Russ spoke for the first time. "You're sure to do well. Are you taking any of your accounts with you?"

"Oh, no," Jenny shook her head. "I want to create my own accounts, because I'll be operating differently from my former company, and—" She fell silent, not wanting to elaborate, then said, "There's really nothing definite about any of it." The truth was, though her project was still in the embryonic stage, she did not want to share all the details with strangers, regardless of how friendly and interested they seemed.

"Well, I want to hear about it later," Steve declared affably. "By the way, when I flew into Bergen yesterday, I reserved a rental car for today. I'd be glad for all of you to join me."

Carla and Russ accepted the invitation at once, and Jenny figured, Why not? She hadn't heard from Kirk, and, besides, she was still counting on meeting him that evening for the folklore show. "Sure, I'd love to."

"Great. You'll love Bergen. I've done my homework." He proceeded to tell her the history of the town.

The conversation was pleasant throughout the meal, and Jenny was fascinated that Steve was so informed. Then the announcement came over the PA system that passengers could start disembarking to go ashore, with a reminder not to forget their boarding passes. "A passenger without a boarding pass," said the clipped but jovial voice, "is a passenger without a ship!"

They laughed, got up, and began to make their way out. Steve was momentarily held back by Miguel's anxious inquiry as to whether he had been satisfied with the service. Jenny kept on going, then, suddenly, her heart was doing cartwheels as she glanced up to see that Kirk, stunning as always in his resplendent uniform, was walking across the dining room in her direction.

"There you are," he greeted, his dazzling smile and devouring gaze blocking out everyone else in the room. "I've been calling your cabin all morning. I wanted to ask if you'd like to go ashore with me today." He was about to ask whether she had seen the note he'd left beside the bed when Steve suddenly reached her side.

Jenny was about to say yes, she'd love to, forgetting all about Steve, but Steve quickly, sharply, interjected, "She's going ashore with us. We already have plans."

Kirk waited for Jenny to confirm, and she could only shrug and say, "That's right. If you'd asked sooner . . ."

Hadn't she seen the note? He struggled to keep smiling. "Okay. I guess I need the time with my family anyway. But I'll see you for the folklore show at five-thirty, right?" he added hopefully.

"Of course." She felt like she was drowning again, felt a warm rush, and wanted to step into his arms then and there. It was all flashing before her, the wonder of his lovemaking, how she had so easily, eagerly, responded. And, she had to secretly admit, she would not mind a repeat performance! "Five-thirty."

He turned, and left by the side exit. Everyone continued on their way.

Jenny did not see the disapproving look on Steve Gentry's face as he turned his head slightly to watch Kirk's departure. Neither did she notice the sudden resentment and anger flashing in his eyes.

____

SEVEN

The rental car, a sleek Volvo, was waiting for them on the pier. Carla and Russ got in the back, and Jenny sat next to Steve in front. "You can be the navigator," he told her, handing her a city map of Bergen. "I know where I want to take us, but you need to read me directions on how to get there."

Once they were settled in and on their way, Carla said to Steve, ignoring Russ's critical glare, "So, what brings you to Norway?"

"Vacation," he replied breezily. "Totally. Absolutely. It's been a busy year. An eventful year. I needed a vacation to recharge my batteries," he added with a chuckle.

Carla, in openhearted candor, wanted to know why he was traveling alone. "I mean . . ." she paused, finally realizing Russ was annoyed with her and thought maybe she *was* being a bit nosy.

"Actually," he continued with ease, not seeming to mind at all that the conversation had become personal, "I *have* been married. In fact, my divorce was part of my eventful year. This is my first time to cut loose in nearly fifteen years.''

"Any children?'' Jenny asked pleasantly.

At that, his whole face seemed to ignite with joy as he quickly reached for his wallet to produce a picture of a smiling little boy. "Steve Junior,'' he announced with fatherly pride, handing it to Jenny to be passed around the car. "We call him Stevie. He's almost three.''

"He's precious,'' Jenny acknowledged, handing the wallet back to Carla, who looked, smiled, agreed with her, then eagerly flipped through the rest of the pictures. She held up one of a pretty young woman with laughing blue eyes and golden-red hair. "Your ex or your girlfriend?''

Russ groaned. "Really, Carla!''

Defensively, she countered, "Well, he didn't say we couldn't look at the rest of the pictures, and she's *pretty*.''

Steve cheerily assured, "Yes, she is, *and . . .*'' he added pointedly, for Russ's benefit, "it was quite all right for you to look at all the pictures. To answer your question, Deborah is actually *both*.''

Carla shook her head. "I don't understand.''

"Ex *and* girlfriend. We had a friendly divorce,'' Steve explained nonchalantly, taking the wallet as she passed it over and putting it away. "No hard feelings.''

"Does she have custody of Stevie?'' Carla wanted to know.

"We *both* have custody. As I said, it was all quite amiable. We're going to raise him together, even though we aren't married to each other. He'll divide his time between us through the years. We're both mature. And, as I said, we're good friends. We'll be able to handle it, and Stevie won't suffer from a broken home as so many children do these days.''

Jenny said she thought that was a wonderful idea, and

then Carla, upset by the way Russ was scowling, offered an apology for being so inquisitive.

"Oh, but that's all right," Steve told her firmly. "You know, Deborah and I used to go on a cruise nearly every year. We were married fifteen years before we had Stevie. And one of the things we loved about cruising was how friendly people can be in just a short period of time. We made some good friends. We even went to visit some of them; they came to see us. And after every cruise I think our Christmas card list grew by a couple of dozen names and addresses."

"Well, I don't think it's right to go on a vacation and have to answer a lot of questions about your personal life," Russ snapped irritably. "After all, that's why you *go* on vacation, to get away from your problems."

Jenny, exchanging a secret smile with Steve, could not resist quipping, "Well, none of *us* seem to have any, Russ."

At that, he lapsed into a stony silence.

Jenny was enjoying her day, for Steve was marvelous company. Witty, bright, delighting in the world around him, he made a perfect companion for sightseeing. She was sad, however, to see that Carla was oblivious to everything around her except Russ. Russ, meanwhile, basked in the way she clung to his arm and hung adoringly onto his every word.

They had a little time left for shopping and visited Bergen's largest department store—Sundt's. Russ and Carla disappeared, saying they would meet them back at the car.

Steve teasingly asked Jenny if she were going to buy herself a pair of reindeer slippers. Horrified, she cried, "Wear Rudolph on my feet? Never!"

And they both convulsed in laughter at the thought.

Instead, she bought colorful, hand-knit sweaters for herself and her parents, and could not pass up a set of hand-crafted Norwegian-pine bookends.

"Let's get out of here," she wailed, noting that Steve had filled two shopping bags with mittens and socks for his family. "We've got lots more ports to visit, remember?" Secretly, she was wanting to hurry back to the ship to have time to dress for her date with Kirk—a long soaking bath, maybe a glass of cold champagne from room service to sip as she dreamed of the evening ahead.

When they reached the parking lot, Carla and Russ were nowhere in sight. "We're a few minutes early," Steve said, loading their shopping bags in the trunk. "No need to worry about them yet."

They got in, and Steve seized the private moment to say confidently, "I want you to know I had a wonderful day, Jenny. You're marvelous company. Just the kind of woman I've been looking for."

She was taken aback by his unexpected remark, could only murmur, "Well, that's nice. I had a good time, too."

He gave an exaggerated sigh. "It's a jungle out there. I never knew it'd be so rough to be single again. It's hard to find an attractive woman who's also intelligent, with a mind of her own. Like *you* . . ." His voice trailed as he gave her a meaningful look.

Again, she could only murmur a small thank-you for the strange compliment.

Suddenly, bluntly, he declared, "I heard you broke up with that lawyer. Are you seeing anyone special now?"

She blinked, surprised that he knew so much about her. "How'd you know about that?"

He shrugged, flashed a confident grin. "I told you I'd heard that Cuisine Unlimited was losing their number-one agent, and there was some speculation that it might be due to your getting married. Then I heard the wedding was off, and you were striking out on your own. So," he repeated, "are you seeing anyone special now?"

She wondered with silent amusement whether sleeping with Kirk the night before meant she was "seeing" him. She knew she wasn't going to divulge anything about her personal life anyway. She shook her head. "No. I only broke up with Bryan a few weeks ago. Atlanta must not be as big as I thought it was. Word sure travels fast."

"Especially when you travel in the fast lane," he said with a teasing wink. Then his demeanor became sober, serious, and he turned in the seat to stare at her thoughtfully for a few seconds before declaring, "I guess you know by now that I'm not the sort to beat around the bush, Jenny. I say what's on my mind, and I want you to know that I like you. A lot. I'd like to get to know you better. Here. On the cruise. Back home. In Atlanta. I think we've got a lot in common. I think we'd be good for each other. At least I'd like to find out. What do you say?"

Jenny shook her head to clear it. Talk about a fast mover! "Well . . ." she hedged, not really knowing what to say. He seemed to be an okay guy, and maybe it would be fun to get to know him better, but for now there was Kirk, and she wanted to just concentrate on the splendor of him for the remainder of the cruise. "Let's just take it one day at a time."

Not about to be dissuaded, he cheerily suggested, "Or one *night* at a time. I know you're seeing that 'white wolf' at five-thirty, but I thought after dinner, we could see what's on the agenda, maybe go to a variety show, dancing later. What do you say?"

Jenny had not heard anything he'd said beyond the obviously derisive description of officers in general. "What do you mean, 'white wolf'?" she wanted to know.

He gave a condescending sneer. "Oh, surely you've

heard that before, Jenny. This isn't your first cruise, is it? Like I said earlier, my ex-wife and I went on lots of cruises, and I can't remember one where we didn't see some slick officer squiring around some dewy-eyed young girl who couldn't see past the uniform. That's why they're called white wolves, because that's what they are—wolves in white uniforms. I know, because my sister went on a cruise once and her heart was broken by an officer, but I'm hoping you're smart enough to realize these guys are only out for one thing, and—"

"Wait a minute!" Jenny cried sharply, holding up a hand in indignant protest. "No, I haven't heard about any white wolves, and what happened to your sister has nothing to do with me."

He frowned, slightly annoyed by her censure. "I'm only giving you my opinion, Jenny. Most of those guys are married, anyway. They're just out for a good time."

"I still think you're being unfair and judgmental."

He stiffened, then snapped, "You don't strike me as the type to be out for just a good time."

She shook her head in wonder. "Steve, you don't know me well enough to categorize me, and I don't appreciate your trying to. Besides, I don't feel I have to justify myself to you or anyone else."

He was contrite, his features softening as he sought to redeem himself. "I'm sorry. I truly am. I had no right to say anything to you about it anyway. I guess I just liked you from the start and got a little jealous to find out you were maybe involved with one of those guys. Friends?" He held out a hand.

Jenny turned her head to look out the window, relieved to at last see that Carla and Russ were coming back. She wanted to end the tense moment. "There's no need," she said, ignoring his outstretched hand. "Let's forget it."

"Then you'll go out with me tonight?" he wanted to know.

"We'll see."

"Jenny, I meant what I said," he persisted. "I like you a lot. And I think it was fated that we'd meet this way. Both of us from Atlanta. Your kind of work fitting in with mine. We both know the same people, probably go to the same clubs. We've got so damn much in common. I warn you, I'm not going to let you get away."

She turned to look at him then, thought he looked like an eager little boy waiting in line to go to the circus. "Like I said," she firmly repeated. "We'll see."

Carla and Russ got in, smiling mysteriously, then Carla could contain herself no longer and cried, "Look what we bought ourselves!" She held up her wrist to flash a beautiful watch.

Likewise, Russ showed off his.

"I'm impressed," Jenny said, then could not resist asking why they bought them here. "Norway isn't known for being a bargain when it comes to watches," she pointed out.

There was a coldness in Russ's eyes as he arrogantly snapped, "We wanted a souvenir of our time together here. We weren't looking for bargains."

Jenny settled in her seat, and told herself for the umpteenth time it was none of her business. Still, she strongly doubted Russ had paid for Carla's watch, and could only hope she had not paid for *his,* too.

When they got back to the ship, Jenny thanked Steve for the pleasant day, and offered to pay her part of the gas. He declined. She noticed Russ took off without making a similar offer, Carla close on his heels. She wasted no time in taking her leave, either. She told Steve she would see him at dinner and rushed off, not giving him time to argue.

She had the suite to herself after Carla dumped her

shopping bags and purse on the bed and said she was joining Russ for drinks in one of the lounges.

After the delicious bath and champagne Jenny had promised herself, she started getting dressed. She chose a simple white dress—scoop-necked, softly pleated, pearl buttons at the long-sleeved cuffs. She felt it was the perfect style for any occasion. Stepping into matching leather pumps, she ran a brush through her hair, slipped on pearl earrings, dabbed on her Giorgio Red this time, was ready to walk out the door, just as it opened and Carla breezed in.

"Forgot my purse, and I need my credit card," she called gaily. "We ran up quite a tab in the bar, and I still haven't got around to registering at the purser's desk."

Jenny stared after her, the words ringing in her ears; *'We ran up quite a tab.'* Was she paying for his drinks? "See you later," she called finally, tightly.

At five-thirty, Jenny stepped off the elevator in front of the main ballroom door and fought the impulse to just sigh out loud at the sight of Kirk standing there waiting for her. He was wearing his day uniform, short-sleeved white shirt, trousers, no coat or tie, black-and-gold bars on his shoulders—and he was *gorgeous!*

He smiled as Jenny approached, and she was well aware of other women nearby, watching in envy.

"So how did you like my hometown?" he greeted, holding out his hand to her.

"Beautiful," she told him with sincerity. "If all of Norway is as lovely, I may never leave."

"Well, I can't wait to show you around at a few of the other ports."

"I'll look forward to it. I'm sorry about today. I really would've liked to go with you."

He told her about the note, then said, "I found it on the floor. I guess it fell off the table and you didn't see it. I rang the cabin just before six, but there wasn't an answer."

"I was in a hurry to change and get up on deck."

He caressed her with his eyes, and she felt the familiar ripple of excitement move over her whole body as he leaned close to whisper, "Last night was wonderful, Jenny. I've thought of nothing else all day."

"I . . . I enjoyed it, too," she managed to say, despite the butterflies in her throat. Then, attempting to quell the intensity of the moment, she rushed to change the subject. "When do you think you'll have time to show me around the ship? I can't forget why I'm here, you know," she added with a soft laugh.

"Tomorrow. We'll be at sea, and I'll have some free time in the afternoon."

They went inside and found a table. After giving their order for two cups of coffee to the waiter, Kirk told her she was in for a real treat at their next port of call, which was Honningsvag, the *Nordkappe,* or North Cape. The huge cliff was called *Ultima Thule,* he explained, which meant the very edge of the North. It dropped straight down into the Arctic Ocean and was once believed to be where the world actually ended. From the first of May to the middle of August, the sun did not set, but turned on the horizon and moved upward again. "Land of the Midnight Sun," he said. "Something you never forget."

And Jenny sensed, as their eyes met and held in a sensuous, melding gaze, that Kirk Moen was also something, *someone,* she would never forget.

"If I can arrange some time off, would you like to go with me to the Cape?"

"I'd love to," she said, just as the lights dimmed and a spotlight fell on a platform that had been placed on the ballroom floor.

He squeezed her hand, flashed one of his melting

smiles, then turned to sign the tab as the waiter brought their coffee.

A middle-aged woman wearing the costume of a Scandinavian peasant stepped up to a microphone and started talking about mythical trolls.

Jenny leaned closer to Kirk and asked, "Do you believe in trolls?"

He laughed. "Of course! All Norwegians believe in trolls."

She stared at him in wonder. Surely a grown man did not believe in fairy tales. He had to be joking, and she decided to play along. "Oh, really?" she teased. "Then, no doubt, you've seen them!"

"*Seen* them?" he echoed incredulously. "Why, my dear, I was *married* to one for nearly five years!"

They both laughed then, and Jenny delighted in his sense of humor. No matter he had previously been married, he could look on his past and any feelings of personal failure with wit, and she admired him for that.

When the show ended, they stood up to leave, and it was then that Jenny realized with a start, *and* with a flash of annoyance, that Steve Gentry had been seated behind them the whole time. Ignoring Kirk, he breezily addressed himself to her. "That was fun, wasn't it? Well, I just heard the chimes for second seating, so if you're ready, we'll go on in. I ordered champagne for the whole table."

Jenny did not know what she expected Kirk to do at that point but was disappointed when he merely gave a curt nod, wished her a good evening, and went on his way. Nothing was said about later.

"Ready?" Steve prodded.

Jenny could only nod and take the hand he held out to her. And, staring wistfully after Kirk, the thought flashed once more: *He really does have nice buns!*

EIGHT

Steve was charming at dinner, good company. Carla winked at Jenny several times to let her know she wholeheartedly approved of him. Jenny could not help wishing she could be as endorsing of Carla's choice of men. The more she was around Russ Claiborne, the less she liked him.

After delicious smoked salmon and all the other courses, Jenny could still not resist dessert, especially when it was such a festive occasion. Miguel and the other waiters and busboys paraded around the dining room with flaming baked Alaskas carefully balanced on their heads, all to the rhythmic beat of a steel drum band.

Steve not only generously provided two bottles of Moët for all of them, he insisted on stopping the rolling after-dinner drink cart to buy a round of brandy for their coffee.

"I'm positively stuffed!" Carla cried. "I might have finally got my luggage, but at this rate, nothing in it will fit at the end of the first week of this cruise!"

"Amen!" Jenny quickly agreed. "I think I'm going to have to find time for a session in the gym tomorrow."

"That sounds great," Steve quickly chimed in. "I try

to work out at least three evenings a week at home. I can tell you do, too," he added, brown eyes giving her an admiring sweep.

Carla asked if he lived near a gym, and he said no, but he was going to be building a house in the suburbs in the fall and was planning a special room for weights and other equipment.

"I'd like to see it," she said. "I'm hoping for an invitation to go visit Jenny."

Jenny smiled noncommittally to agree that was a lovely idea, while Steve assured he'd look forward to seeing her again and would take the three of them out to dinner. "Maybe we can even take little Stevie," he fondly added, "if we can keep him up that late."

Jenny thought that an odd notion but didn't say anything. Evidently he was one of those doting parents who liked to include their children in as many of their activities as possible. Well, that was his business. She personally felt there was a time and a place for everything, and taking kids everywhere she went would not be one of her priorities when, and if, she ever had any of her own.

Steve suggested they go to the musical review being staged in the main auditorium. Jenny agreed, knowing she needed to experience everything on the ship.

"How about you two?" Steve asked of Carla and Russ.

Carla looked to Russ, who quickly dashed her hopes by glancing at his new watch and saying, "The casino just opened. We're heading there."

"Maybe," Jenny dared to interject, "you'd like to come with us and meet Russ later."

Smugly, Russ answered for her. "No. She's my good-luck charm. I need her with me."

Yeah, Jenny silently and cynically, mused. *She's probably your gambling stake, too!*

* * *

The show was enjoyable, and, afterward, Steve suggested wine and dancing in one of the ballrooms. "I heard the band there plays music for slow dancing."

"Don't you like to fast dance?" Jenny asked.

"Not really. Oh, back in my college days, it was the Shag . . . beach music. You know. I doubt we'll find any of that on board this ship."

"They probably play all kinds of music in the disco. It stays open till three in the morning."

"I'd fall asleep on my feet. Could you really stay up so late?" he asked incredulously.

She assured she could, and often did. "I'm a night person. I think I must have a little vampire in me, because I come alive when it gets dark."

"Really?" He did not sound impressed. "I guess that's what comes from being used to married life. Deborah and I had kind of a quiet life. We'd go out to a club with friends once in a while, but mostly we enjoyed staying home, cooking on the grill, having people over. Especially after Stevie was born," he added with the sudden glow that came on his face every time he mentioned his son.

"Well, there's nothing wrong with that," Jenny conceded. "Maybe when I get married, I'll settle down like that, too, but I sure don't intend to gather any moss till I have to. Life is too short, my friend."

"Well, then . . ." He slipped his arm around her shoulders casually as they walked along the enclosed international deck. "How about if we have some fun now? I really want to dance with you."

"And I love to dance, like I said, but I like all kinds of dancing, so how about if we go to the disco?" She had glanced in on the other lounges the evening before, knew they were frequented mostly by the older passengers. That was fine. She heartily approved of entertainment planned for all age groups, and intended to mention that feature in her brochure. But, for herself, she wanted to go where the action was.

Steve smiled only with his lips, for his eyes were coldly brooding. Tightly, he said, "Sure," then led the way to the stairs that would take them two decks below to the disco.

It was crowded, noisy, smoky, and *wonderful*, Jenny decided the instant they walked in. A whirling glass ball dazzled the room with millions of tiny lights and the dance floor was covered in mirrors.

Steve strained to be heard over the din. "I don't think we can even find a place to sit," he said loudly and dubiously, "and I sure don't care to perch on a bar stool."

"Over there!" Jenny spotted a booth in a corner and took off with him right behind her.

The music playing had a wonderful beat, and she was dying to dance, but Steve merely sat there looking miserable. He ordered two white wines, and Jenny took a sip, decided house vintage was terrible. Then it didn't matter anymore, because she was not about to sit and sip all evening. A young man sitting at the next booth, whose wife was as unenthusiastic as Steve, asked her to dance. He was good, and so was she, and they danced well together. One song ended. Another began. There was a break, and her partner's wife smiled and said she was glad her husband had found someone to party with, because she was tired and glad to sit on the sidelines and just watch. Jenny suggested they move to their booth, and they did. A pitcher of beer was ordered and then, Joe, he'd said his name was, urged her onto the floor, and the happy madness began all over again.

The music played on, and Jenny was tired but having too much fun to quit. Finally, though, at around one in the morning, Joe's wife apologetically announced she'd had it. She was turning in for the night, and made it obvious with a meaningful look in her husband's direction that he was expected to retire, too. No way was she leaving him alone in the disco.

After they had gone, Steve bluntly said he was relieved. "How can I impress you with what a great guy I am if you stay on the dance floor with someone else?"

"Well, I'm glad to sit for a while," she told him pleasantly. "So go ahead. Impress me," she lightly teased.

He talked some about himself, Stevie, his work, then began to field questions to her, which she sidestepped as much as possible. Then he said he had passes to the Falcons' home football games, and she gave a tentative promise to go with him to the season opener. "Maybe we'll even take Stevie," he said, searching her eyes for her reaction.

Absently, she said that might be nice, but could not help wondering why a man would want to take a child not yet three years old to a football game, especially if he had a date.

"I'm looking forward to going ashore with you at our next port—the North Cape," he continued to push.

"Well, I have other plans . . . I *think*," she added thoughtfully, dreamily wondering when she would hear from Kirk again.

Steve continued to almost shout in her ear above the music, wanting to establish their time together for the remainder of the cruise. She was listening only half-heartedly. True, he *was* nice, and she was well aware of the envious glances from unattached girls around them. Jenny had not been aware there were that many, but then it was a large ship, could accommodate nearly eighteen hundred passengers, and it was only natural the younger set would be in the disco at such an hour.

And she could not help watching the officers that stood at the bar. Resplendent in their dress white uniforms, the girls flirted and the officers responded. Matches were made, or those already begun continued. Was it true what Steve said about the so-called "white wolves?" She could not help wondering.

She looked at her watch. Nearly two A.M. She was not really tired, was actually enjoying the music, and Steve was turning out to be good company.

Steve was watching her intently, wishing he could read her thoughts. He wanted to ask her to dance and would do so just as soon as the DJ played a slow song. The music always became slower, he knew, when the night wore on and people began to think about leaving together. Soon, he wanted to reach that stage in their growing relationship—dancing close in each other's arms—but there were still a few things he wanted to find out about her, and he needed more time to chat. "How about another white wine?" he offered. "I'm not much of a beer drinker myself, not really much of a drinker at all." He signaled to the waiter.

She was about to tell him that would be nice, only this time, she preferred coffee and with a splash of cream and Kahlua. "Yes, but instead—"

She fell silent, because, suddenly—he was there.

Tall, powerfully built, golden hair gleaming in the swirling lights, fjord-blue eyes transmitting secret messages of desire, Jenny was later to dreamily recall it was like seeing a mystical Viking, only one wearing the uniform of a Norwegian officer, and, instead of being terrified, she brashly, eagerly, welcomed ravishment.

Jenny knew, without a doubt, that if she lived to be ninety years old and wound up sitting in a rocking chair in a rest home looking back on her life, she would never forget the song that was playing at that particular moment in time; sexy and sensuous Julio Iglesias was singing "When I Fall in Love."

Kirk held out his hand, and his impassioned voice was like a mesmeric caress when he asked, "Would you like to dance?"

She stood and moved into the eager arms he held out to her.

The world around them dissipated as they entered an abysmal sphere all their own, lost in the music, the night, and each other.

Julio finished his song, then Barbra Streisand began to sing of memories. But she was only into her second verse when Kirk glanced over the top of Jenny's head to meet the glaring eyes of the man he had whisked her away from. "If looks could kill, I'd be dead. Who is he?"

"Just a guy who sits at the same table as me in the dining room." She saw no reason to confide that Steve Gentry obviously wanted to be much more.

"Well, he acted rather possessive after the folklore show, and that's why I decided it was best that I leave when I did. There is always criticism from single male passengers who come on board and find officers taking up too much time with single ladies. Frankly, I wasn't even supposed to ask you to dance while you were sitting with him."

"That's ridiculous."

"I guess it's all in how you look at it. He pays to have a good time, then finds himself all alone while you're out here dancing with me. To him, that isn't fair."

Jenny said she didn't care, because, at that particular moment in time, she didn't care about anything in the whole wide world, except Kirk's arms around her, moving her dreamily around the dance floor.

"Would you meet me on deck in a few minutes?" he suddenly asked, drawing back to stare intensely at her to gauge her reaction. "Get your purse and meet me by the pool bar?"

"Well, yes . . ." she said hesitantly. "But—"

"I want to be with you, Jenny," he said tersely, suddenly pulling her against him, and she could feel his desire as she was feeling her own. "I can't walk out of here with you. Your friend over there might run straight to the captain and complain and I'd be in for a lecture."

She understood. They danced till the music ended, then he led her back to her table and left her with a polite thank-you for the dance and an amiable nod for Steve's blazing eyes.

Steve could not contain his rage. "White Wolf!" he all but snarled. "Probably married and has kids, and all he cares about is having a different woman in his bed every cruise. Disgusting."

No, Jenny silently told him, *he's not married and he doesn't have kids, and, frankly, it doesn't matter if I am in his bed for just this cruise, because he makes me feel like a real woman, and damn it, that's what I need right now!*

He kept on grumbling, pointing out officers at the bar flirting with women, and made a snide remark when a couple left together. Finally, Jenny could stand it no longer, all she wanted was to rush into Kirk's wonderful arms. "I think I'll call it a day." She stood, gathered her purse. "Thanks for the evening. I enjoyed it."

"But . . . but I was going to ask you to dance," he sputtered in disbelief. "And you said you liked to stay out late, and—"

"I really am tired tonight, Steve."

He leaped to his feet, signaling frantically to the waiter to bring the check so he could settle up. "Wait. I'll walk you to your cabin. You have a suite, don't you? We can order sandwiches from room service if you like, some coffee, talk, get to know each other better, and—"

He was frantic, almost hysterical, and Jenny thought

that was sad, but it did not change her mind. "Good night, Steve," she said firmly. "See you for breakfast." And she hurried out, leaving him standing there still waving for the waiter.

She made her way through the main hallway, took an elevator five decks up to poolside. The doors opened, and Kirk was there waiting for her, to draw her quickly into his arms then and there. No one else was around, and he kissed her for long, feverish moments, then tenderly murmured, "I missed you, Jenny. It's seemed like forever since I held you."

"Then hold me," she brazenly urged. "Hold me all night long . . ."

He took her hand and hurriedly led the way.

Once in his cabin, with the door securely locking them away from the world, she reached up to twine her arms around his neck, standing on tiptoe to press her lips to his mouth. She felt him shudder, returning her kiss as though he wished to steal her very soul. Suddenly, with a single, easy movement, he swung her up off her feet, mouth never leaving hers as he carried her once more to the bedroom.

He set her down then, standing so close together they could feel each other's heated breath. By mutual, silent agreement, they began to tear off their clothes in near frantic movements. He reached to cup her breasts at the same time she clutched his buttocks to pull him closer, rising on tiptoe once more, this time so that his hard shaft could slide between her thighs. She rode him momentarily, then withdrew, for the feeling was too intense, too soon. She felt the heat of his skin, reveling in it, the rough abrasion of his body hair pressed against her belly.

Together they fell onto the bed, and he wrapped his arms around her, coming down on top of her so that her heaving breasts were crushed by the weight of his strong, broad chest. She caught her breath at the feel of his mouth against her neck, suckling gently, down her chest, to her breasts, taking each nipple in turn. Her fingers wrapped in his thick hair as he maneuvered downward.

She gasped out loud with delight as his tongue began to circle her navel, then left a trail of fire as he suddenly plunged downward. With one quick jerk, he had her thighs apart, then burrowed his mouth, his tongue, in her most velvet recesses. The gasp became a moan, almost a scream, and she turned her face into the pillow to burrow and silence her enraptured cries as he continued to hungrily devour her. She felt his tongue up inside her, *within* her, and she thought surely she would die from the hot needles of raw, savage pleasure that tore through her loins.

She could stand no more. She spread her legs wide, reached for him, her fingers wrapping about his strong, pulsating organ at the same time she maneuvered his face from between her thighs. She guided him into her, and she quivered at the feel of him, and he came inside her, hot, hard, wonderful, enormous. She cried out loud, and he silenced her with a bruising kiss, her nails digging into the back of his neck.

He drove deep, hard, and she raised her legs higher to wrap around his waist so she could take more of him. His mouth left hers to lick hot kisses along her neck, and she kissed his ear, his cheek, as he drove into her relentlessly.

''Jenny, Jenny, oh, dear God,'' he growled, fighting to hold back his own rush of climax.

She felt it coming, that overwhelming shudder. ''Now!'' she commanded, fiercely undulating her hips to meet his driving powerful thrust. ''Now, Kirk, now. Come with me, please . . .''

And he did, trembling and shuddering and stiffening and fighting his own frenzied cries from deep, deep within. Then, finally, he collapsed on top of her, breath warm against her neck, still clutching her tightly against him, sweat-damp bodies clinging together as of one flesh.

Slowly, they returned to the world they had so quickly soared away from.

With a deep sigh of finality and weariness, Kirk rolled to one side, but he continued to hold her, cradling her head against his shoulder as he tenderly stroked her hair. "Wonderful," he whispered huskily. "I never knew it could be so good. You're a hell of a woman, Jenny Denton, and I'm not going to let you go."

She could not help softly laughing to remind him that he didn't even know her. "You don't really know anything about me, Kirk," she said.

"I'm willing to take time to find out," he assured her. "And I've got a feeling I'm going to like everything I learn."

She snuggled her head against his shoulder, liking the protected way he made her feel. "Is that possible on a cruise?" she suddenly challenged. "To find out what a person is *really* like, when everything is such a fantasy?"

"We can try. Besides, I'm thinking about *after*. We dry dock in Germany for a month, then I go on leave for eight weeks. We could see each other then. You come to Norway. I'll visit you in the States . . . *if* you invite me," he added pointedly.

"Sounds good to me," she fervently told him.

He was suddenly quiet, thoughtful, and she sensed there was something on his mind and asked what it was. Finally, he said, "Well, I guess it's only natural I wonder if I've got competition. A beautiful woman like you. Is there somebody in Atlanta waiting for you?"

"No," she easily answered, then could sense his doubt so told him, as briefly as possible, about her broken engagement.

"So I have to compete with the ghost of the past?" he asked soberly.

"Only if you think I envision you as Bryan when we're making love."

For an instant he could only stare at her in amazement, crushed momentarily that she could say such a thing. Then, reaching for her again, he firmly avowed, "Well, my dear, I guess I'll just have to remind you who you *are* making love to."

And the smoldering ashes of their spent passion ignited once more into the licking flames of ecstasy . . . and soon they left the world once more, lost in each other.

NINE

Sometime before dawn Kirk left her to report for duty. This time when he called the cabin, it was nearly nine o'clock and Jenny was sleeping soundly. "Good morning," he said jovially. "I see I woke you up."

She took one look at her watch and groaned, "I can't believe I slept this late. Good grief, I've got to get out of here."

"No problem really. Just take the Do Not Disturb sign off the door when you leave so my steward can get in to clean."

"What time did you get up?"

"Five-thirty. I went on duty at six. Want to meet me for lunch? Afterward, we can take that tour of the ship I promised."

"Wonderful!" she cried. "I don't think I told you, but I've been invited to a party in Oslo by the Valhalla people, and I'd like to have some notes to show them for what I've got in mind by then.

"So . . ." she then asked. "Where do you want me to meet you?"

"I thought we'd go to officers' mess. Give you an idea of how the other half lives," he said wryly.

"Sounds interesting."

"Meet me back in my cabin at quarter to twelve. I left a spare key for you on the coffee table in case I'm late."

He rang off, and Jenny hurried to find her clothes, which seemed to be scattered all over the place. She felt a warm glow recalling how eagerly they had each stripped the night before. Never, ever, had she felt so uninhibited in a man's arms, had not realized it till now. Kirk just made her feel so . . . so free, and, yes, so wanton, wicked, and *great*!

She glanced around the cabin, thought how lonely a place it was. Everything was so stark, so functional. There were hardly any personal belongings at all. Why, even in college, her dormitory room had seemed homier than this. The life of a sailor was not that glamorous, she decided, figuring Kirk probably shared her opinion.

Remembering to take down the sign Kirk had left hanging on the doorknob, she headed back to her suite.

Carla was just coming out of the shower and cried, "Where have you been? I didn't get in myself till after eight, but Steve's been calling every fifteen minutes. He panicked when you didn't show for breakfast, and he just called five minutes ago and said if you didn't show soon, he was calling security."

Jenny tossed her purse on the bed and stared at her in bewilderment. "Well, did you tell him I wasn't here all night?"

"Of course not," she laughed. "How would I know, anyway? *I* wasn't here. And I wasn't about to tell him that I figured you weren't, either, because your bed hadn't been slept in. But if you weren't out with Steve . . . where were you?" she repeated, dying to find out.

Jenny skirted the question with one of her own. "What,

exactly, did you tell Steve?'' She was more than slightly annoyed at his concern, not to mention his persistence.

''I said I hadn't seen you this morning, that you must've got up before I did and gone for a walk on deck. Then he called back to say he'd been all over the ship and couldn't find you.''

The phone rang just then.

''That'll be him, again,'' Carla quickly said.

''Tell him . . .'' Jenny requested, brushing by her to head for the bathroom. ''Tell him I'm taking a shower, that I have plans for the day, and I'll see him later.''

''Why don't you tell him yourself?''

Jenny turned to smile and wink. ''Because he asks a lot of questions, like somebody else I know, and I don't have time for explanations.''

When she came back out, Carla was sitting on the side of her bed, having just finished painting her nails a bright pink. Without looking up, she related, ''Steve was kind of upset. I think he's really flipped for you.''

''He doesn't even know me. We only met yesterday, for heaven's sake.''

Carla shrugged. ''Well, it happens. Like with me and Russ. We've only known each other a short time, but we both feel we've got a good thing going, and we aren't going to let it end when the cruise does. Have *you* met somebody, too?''

Jenny sighed with resignation. She might as well tell her, because sooner or later she'd see her out somewhere with Kirk anyway. ''Remember the officer at the lifeboat drill?''

Carla gasped, ''You mean the hunk? That gorgeous blond-haired, blue-eyed hunk? *That's* who you're seeing? Oh, Jenny, he's really something!''

''And you aren't to say anything to anybody.'' Jenny

hoped she could trust her, that she was as different from Linda as she hoped Kirk was from Bryan.

"Not a soul." She smiled, happy for her. "I really think this is great."

So do I, Jenny dreamily thought to herself, lying across the bed for a quick nap as Carla prepared to leave to meet Russ. *So do I . . .*

The shrill ringing of the phone woke her up, and Jenny groggily answered. At once, she was annoyed by the obvious indignity she detected in Steve's voice. "*Where* have you been? I have looked all over this ship, which is no small chore! I've been worried to death you'd fallen overboard."

She took a deep breath, counted to ten lest she explode. She began talking slowly, wanting to give herself time to wake up and be completely coherent. "I'm sorry you were upset, but you know you shouldn't be. I did come on this ship to work, too, and I really don't want to be accountable to anyone for my time. *That* is why I don't make definite dates, Steve."

"But we had a date for breakfast," he pointed out, tightly.

"No, we didn't."

"Yes, we did. The last thing you said when you rushed out of the disco last night was that you'd meet me for breakfast. I had every reason to be upset when you didn't show up."

Jenny's sigh was exasperated. "That was not my understanding."

"Well . . ." he made his tone bright, wanting to get things on the right track again, soothe her apparent annoyance with him. "It's lunchtime. Want to meet me in the dining room? We can take in a movie afterward."

Jenny looked at her watch. Twenty till twelve. *Thank*

you for waking me up in time for my date, she silently praised him, then breezily said, "Can't. I've got a business meeting."

There was silence for a moment on his end, then, "Tonight is formal," he finally said. "The captain's cocktail party. How about if we meet for that?"

Jenny did not want to make any promises, because she did not know how the day would go with Kirk, what *he* had in mind for later. "We'll see," she said. "I've really got to go, Steve," she then said, "I'm running late."

Reluctantly, he said good-bye and hung up.

She rushed to the closet, frantically wondering what to wear. A tour of the ship could take her anywhere, so she decided her best bet was slacks, sweater, Reeboks again.

She ran a comb through her hair, repaired her makeup, one quick spritz of Giorgio, and she was on her way.

When she reached Kirk's cabin, she tapped on the door, but there was no answer. She let herself in with the key, had just closed the door and turned around when he stepped from behind the curtain separating the bedroom.

He was wrapping a towel around his waist, and his hair was wet. His broad chest still glistened from his shower, and just the sight of his half-naked body filled her with desire. Sucking in her breath quickly, she managed to speak above the welling desire, "Uh . . . Hi! I knocked, but . . ." She let her voice trail.

"Make yourself at home," he smiled. "Be with you in a minute."

He closed the curtain, went to the closet to take out a fresh uniform. What he *wanted* to do was go in there and lift her in his arms and bring her in here to spend the rest of the afternoon in bed! Again and again, he wanted to remind her she was making love to him, not Bryan what's his name. When she'd said that the night before, he was impressed by her candor but could only hope there was no real problem behind this honest remark.

He had hated to leave her that morning, but he was, after all, working. This was no two-week vacation for him. And it was always difficult to work in a relationship amid his sometimes crazy schedule. This cruise, especially, was more demanding than the usual runs in the Caribbean. Lots of brass on board. Lots more in every port. He had known it would be a busy time. That was why he had told Marla not to come on this cruise when she had written that she planned to. And he was very glad he'd told the radio operator not to ring his room last night, because this morning when he'd got to the bridge, he'd learned Marla had phoned all the way from the States several times during the night. She never cared that her shore-to-ship calls via satellite ticked at a dollar a minute. She had rich parents who indulged her every whim. She was also spoiled rotten, used to getting her own way, and she was the one girl in his life right now he was worried about. Not that he was getting any serious notions about her. Just the opposite. *She* was getting serious notions about *him*. And it did not take a genius to figure out why. He was not accessible. He had let her know, from day one, that he had no intentions of getting seriously involved. Most women were appreciative of such honesty. To Marla, it was just a challenge.

So, he tried to keep things light. For a year or so, she had come on board at least twice during his every four-month tour of duty. He had visited her on his last vacation, enjoyed a week on her father's yacht off the coast of Texas. They had great sex, lots of fun, and that's all he wanted from her . . . all, really, he wanted from any of the women he met on the ship.

Until Jenny Denton.

Now, resolves were melting, intentions forgotten, and he was starting to have the feeling he thought he would never experience again—falling in love.

Suddenly she called to him from the other room. "So tell me, how do you feel? I was able to get a little nap, but you must be dead on your feet."

"Not really." He brushed the curtain aside, smiled at her warmly, felt the familiar rush at just the sight of her. He crossed the room to draw her up into his arms for a kiss that left both of them shaken, then huskily whispered, "You're energizing for me. Like an addiction. And I'm going to have to have a fix every single night of this cruise, believe me."

She swayed in his arms, wishing it were much, much later—and all they had to do was go to bed and make mad, passionate love till dawn. "Well, I'm afraid I have to confess I'm getting a bit hooked, too."

"Great. As long as we both feel the same way."

Their eyes met, held, almost hypnotically, and it was only with great effort that Kirk was able to say, "We'd better get out of here while we still can."

"Right," she agreed in a throaty whisper.

He nodded to the door. "Ready to see how the other half lives?"

Officer's mess was a small room on the very bottom deck. With old, plastered, and patched pipes running overhead, Jenny did not find it a very appealing place. It was crudely and sparsely furnished with plain wood tables and chairs. A neatly uniformed busboy presided over a cloth-covered table offering fresh fruit, cheeses, cold, sliced meat, and an array of hot dishes, not as fancy as in the passenger dining room, but adequate.

Few officers, she noted, were dressed in short-sleeved

white uniforms like Kirk, opting instead for one-piece outfits he explained were called boiler suits.

They sat down with two other officers Kirk introduced as a radio technician and an engineer. They made polite conversation—Jenny inquiring where they were from in Norway, the officers asking her about life in America. It was a friendly, pleasant time, and she enjoyed herself.

After a dessert of creamy rice pudding, a special Norwegian recipe, Kirk confided, they got ready to leave. Just as they reached the door, another officer entered, with a small, blond woman at his side. Jenny looked on as they all exchanged greetings in Norwegian. Kirk introduced her to Mr. Ingebretsen and his wife, Dayna, explaining Dayna spoke hardly any English. She had joined her husband in Bergen but would be leaving the ship at the North Cape to visit awhile with her parents, who lived there.

As he spoke, Jenny thought how awful it must be to have a husband at sea. Four months away, two months home—a couple would have to work hard for quality time together. She knew that when the time came that she did marry, she would not want long periods of separation. That just wasn't what marriage was all about for her. With that thought in mind, she cast a sideways glance at Kirk. Attractive and desirable though he was, she kept telling her heart to remember he was, after all, a sailor.

But her heart did not seem to be listening!

After the tour, they returned to the main deck, where Kirk reluctantly said he would soon have to get back to work. "It's after four, and I've got some paper work to do. Then I've got to get ready for the captain's big party tonight. He wants all his officers present in dress uniform. But . . ." He nodded in the direction of the tea carts being rolled out and set up with their offering of dainty sandwiches and mouth-watering pastries and cookies, "I've got time for a Coke, if you'd like."

"I'd like," she assured him.

They each got a cup, sat down on a bench. He gave her an adoring look and whispered, "You know, I'd much rather take you back to my cabin where we could be alone, but frankly, I don't dare. It's all I can do to keep my hands off of you right now."

"You're wicked!" she said with a wink. "And I love it."

"That's not the only reason I want to be with you," he suddenly felt the need to say. "I like being with you, Jenny. You're fun to be with. Interesting to talk to. Every time we're together, I find more to like and enjoy."

She felt the same way about him and said so.

The sensual tension between them was growing, and Kirk finally took a ragged breath, downed the last of his Coke, and reluctantly got to his feet. "I think I'd better get my mind on something else—like work."

Jenny nodded, wanting desperately to be in his arms and feel his lips crushing down on hers. She also stood, and fervently, hopefully said, "I'll see you tonight?"

He nodded, blue eyes devouring her. "At the cocktail party. Then I've got duty till twelve. Do you still have my key?"

She said she did.

"Well . . ." He gave a slow grin. "It would be real nice to find you in my cabin around midnight. But if you'd rather I came to the disco, I can. It's just that officers are required to wear full dress uniforms in public after eight o'clock, and I'd have to take time to change, and—"

"No need!" She was quick to interrupt. "I'll be there."

He winked, smiled once more, and left her.

Jenny stared after him for a moment, then went to the

windows of the enclosed deck to stare out at the misty gray sea. She needed to go back to her cabin and make notes, start giving some thought as to how she was going to put the brochure presentation together in rough draft for the Valhalla executives in Oslo. But that could wait. For the time being she wanted only to savor the day, remember each and every smile, wink, secret glance, and touch of hand. Kirk was meaning more and more to her with every passing hour, and Jenny found herself wondering where it was all going to lead . . .

She did not see Steve Gentry from where he stood watching, a little way down the deck. Nor had she been aware that he had been observing her while she was sitting with Kirk.

He was frowning, his hands opening and closing in angry fists. He had grown tired of the silly, incompetent women he had encountered in Atlanta since his divorce. All they wanted was a husband, someone to take care of them. Well, maybe he admitted to looking for a wife, someone to be a mother to Stevie during the times his son would be living with him, a mother to afford the child a well-rounded life. But the fact was, Steve wanted more than that in a wife. He wanted someone mature, intelligent, someone who could balance a career and marriage and motherhood. When he had met Jenny, he'd known at once she was the one he'd been searching for. And how ironic that she was from Atlanta!

Yes, he thought with satisfaction, she was perfect. And also very beautiful—an added bonus.

His fists clenched and unclenched once more as the anger flashed over him again.

He was not going to lose out to a *white wolf*.

No doubt, he rationalized, Jenny was reacting to being on the rebound after her broken engagement. She was merely, though she probably did not even realize it herself, having a rebellious fling, not thinking of the folly of her actions . . . or possible consequences.

But Steve was going to do her a favor.

He was going to find a way to make her realize she was making a mistake and see that *he* was the right man for her.

He would stop at nothing to accomplish that goal!

TEN

Jenny turned in front of the full-length mirror, liking the effect of the Oleg Cassini evening gown. Black silk, hand-stitched with bronze-and-gold-tone sequins, there was an all-over scattering of tiny beads. The chemise shape flared into graceful pleats at the hem, and the back was open. She debated over which shoes to wear—golden brocade pumps with black velvet heels or plain gold metallic leather—and finally, opted for the plain. Her only jewelry were earrings—gold twisted rims adorned with jet-black pavé crystals.

With hot rollers, hair spray, and great patience, she had turned her shoulder-length hair into glamorous spirals all over her head.

Yes, she thought with satisfaction, she liked the effect, and felt sure Kirk would also.

Kirk.

Just thinking his name created an excited rush. What was happening to her? In so short a time, he meant so very much to her. She had never given much credence to love at first sight but only because it had never happened to her. Now she was beginning to wonder if it might really be possible. He spoke of the future, as though this were not just a shipboard romance, and they weren't really like ships that pass in the night.

Yes, Jenny thought with a peaceful sigh, it was all quite wonderful, maybe *too* wonderful to be true, but, for the moment, she was going to enjoy it all!

Carla came in, and gasped out loud. "Gorgeous! Positively, drop-dead gorgeous! You look like a movie star!"

"Thanks," Jenny said, then, noting the time, urged her cabinmate to get dressed. "The cocktail party starts at seven, and it's ten till," she reminded her.

Carla dashed around the room, pulling out stockings, slip, underwear. "Is this okay?" she asked.

She held up a creation in pink sequins that Jenny assured looked very nice.

"I borrowed it from my cousin. She bought it for a cruise she went on last year, so I figured it'd be okay. I didn't know *what* to buy. Not that I couldn't afford to buy new stuff. I mean, I might've wound up with a broken heart and feeling like a fool, but Robbie *did* give me a good enough settlement that I'm not going to have to worry about money for a while. I guess he felt guilty, knowing I was hoping we'd work things out, get back together, and the whole time he was having an affair, planning to get married as soon as the divorce was final. But I've got a lot to be thankful for, and now there's Russ. Who'd have thought I would find somebody so soon?" She headed for the shower, calling over her shoulder, "You'd better go on without me. I'm supposed to meet Russ anyway. We're running late; he had a streak of bad luck in the casino, and if they hadn't closed down till after dinner, he'd still be there trying to win it back."

Jenny hoped once more that Carla wasn't headed for a big fall. She was suddenly struck with the awareness that even her cynicism for girlfriends was fading, thanks to her own newfound happiness. *This cruise*, she thought with a smile, aware of admiring glances as she made her way to the party, *was turning out to be wonderful in many, many ways!* She knew she'd been well on her way to becoming a bitter woman, but all that had changed, thank goodness. Now she was optimistic about the future, and regrets of the past were fading more and more with each passing day.

In the hallway leading to the ballroom, there was a receiving line, where the ship's hostess introduced passengers to the captain as a photographer snapped a quick souvenir photo. Jenny shook the captain's hand, found him quite nice and charming, then moved on.

A waiter came by offering a choice of Manhattans, daiquiris, white wine, or champagne. Jenny opted for champagne, sipping the cold bubbles as she glanced around in search of an empty table.

"Jenny, here!"

She saw Steve frantically waving from where he stood beside a table right next to the ballroom floor.

"Over here! I saved this table for us!"

She headed in that direction but without enthusiasm. She had wanted to find her own table, near the floor, in hopes that when the formalities were over, Kirk would come and sit with her. They could have a drink together, maybe dance before time for second seating dinner. But she remembered him saying he had a lot of work to do this evening, probably, she supposed, in anticipation of their arrival at the North Cape the next day. He would, no doubt, leave early. So she pacified her disappointment with the thought that Steve was not bad company, if he would just stop pushing so hard for a relationship beyond casual friendship.

"My God!" His eyes raked over her in appreciative

wonder, stammering, "You . . . you are absolutely the most beautiful woman I've ever seen, Jenny! I'm . . . I'm speechless!"

"Good!" she said, sliding into the booth and suddenly feeling embarrassed. "Please sit down. People are staring."

He moved to sit close beside her, unable to take his eyes off her. "I can't help myself. You're gorgeous!"

"Try," she said between gritted teeth, "or I'm going to find somewhere else to sit! Thank you for your compliments, Steve, but you're making a scene, and I really don't relish being the center of attention!"

He took a deep breath, "Okay. So . . ." He flashed a grin at her, happy over her nearness. "How was your business meeting this afternoon? Everything go okay?" He was not about to let her know that he knew where she'd been or *whom* she had been with. Not then, anyway.

"Yes, fine." She nodded amiably. "It was all very informative."

"You're really enthused over this project, aren't you? Getting the PR contract for Valhalla Lines?"

"Yes. They're not getting the exposure they need to compete with the other cruise lines. It's so obvious that with the right promotion, it'll be a piece of cake to get them right up there with the rest of them, maybe even make theirs the leading ships."

"I've heard you've done that with every account you've ever worked on," he said with admiration. "Taken each and every one right to the top. So I don't think there's any reason not to believe you won't do it with Valhalla. Have you got an idea in mind for another account after you land this one?"

She finished her champagne, and he reached for another glass from a passing waiter. Then she explained that she hadn't had time to research the market, make comparisons on other businesses. "All of this happened rather suddenly. Not exactly overnight, because I'd been dissatisfied where I was for some time. But I haven't really had the time to plan my strategy. I'll just have to take it one account at a time."

"I was thinking about your not having an office yet," Steve interjected, "and I thought maybe you'd be interested in sharing space with me. I lease a small building in a complex on the east side with easy access off I-285. Not very large, but there's a big reception area, and my secretary only uses half of it. There's room for another. And there's an empty room besides the one I use for my office. You could set up there till you get on your feet. The idea of an architect and a public relations firm sharing an office isn't inconceivable."

No, Jenny silently agreed, it wasn't, and the idea was appealing. She knew where his complex was; an ideal location. Good parking. Good visibility. But would Steve be able to keep things to a strictly business relationship or would he think his generosity gave him special privileges? She'd need time to think about that, see how the rest of the cruise went. Finally, she said, "Well, we'll have to look into it when we got home. It sounds nice, Steve."

"It *will* be," he said assuredly. "We'll get along real well together, I'm sure. You're my kind of woman, Jenny Denton!"

He winked, reached for her hand and squeezed, but she discreetly pulled it back as the soft lights of the ballroom suddenly came up.

The band started playing a stirring marching song as an impressive group of men in sharp white uniforms began to file in. Jenny felt a thrilling rush as she recognized Kirk, and he seemed to be glancing around the room in search of her. *He was!* His eyes fell on her and he smiled broadly. She was not aware of the way Steve stiffened as he, also, took note of the awareness between the two.

The officers lined up in a semicircle, and then Captain Ulland was introduced by the cruise director over a microphone. Stepping into a dramatic spotlight as a respectful hush came over the audience, he greeted in his rich accent, "*Velkommen!*" then proceeded to give his welcoming speech.

Next, he started introducing his staff of officers, and each stepped forward in turn as their title and names were called.

When he announced, "My Chief Officer Senior—Kirk Moen," Jenny felt so proud and happy. This was the man who had made her feel like a real woman for the first time in her life. This was the man who made her feel vibrant, alive, as though she could climb the highest mountain as long as he was at her side. This was, she realized with almost frightening clarity, the man she just might be falling in love with!

When the festivities ended, the officers began to mingle among the passengers. The band began to play dance music. Jenny saw she was right in predicting that Kirk would have to report for duty when she saw him leaving by a side exit. As Steve got to his feet, she remarked, "They haven't rung the chimes for second-seating."

He held out his hand to her. "I need to stop by the gift shop, pick up some toothpaste. Walk with me, please."

She thought he seemed a bit—what? Anxious? Nervous? Whatever, she decided to go along, remembering she needed to get an extra roll of film for the North Cape.

There were not many people in the gift shop, and Jenny immediately selected her film and took it to a register where there was not a line. Just as she was handing it to the cashier, Steve suddenly snatched it from her hand to say, "No, come back here to the register where I'm ringing up."

Bewildered, aware the cashier was also staring at him curiously, Jenny followed him to the back of the shop. A smiling uniformed clerk was waiting. Steve surprised Jenny further by introducing her. "This is my friend, Jenny Denton, from Atlanta. Same place as me," he said, as though he were very proud of that fact. Then, "Jenny, this is Paula Streeter. She's from England. She's worked on this ship for nearly two years now. Isn't that something?"

Jenny murmured yes, it was, wondering if Steve was trying to make her jealous. If so, it wasn't working. She took her wallet from her bag, ready to pay for the film when Paula Streeter got around to ringing it up, not about to let Steve do so.

"Paula says cruise ship life is very fascinating," he said then. "Isn't that so, Paula?"

In a very distinct cockney accent, Paula eagerly assured, "Oh, yes, luv. You'd be surprised at what goes on on a cruise ship. I've seen it all. The tales I could tell. One day I'm going to write a book, I am. Tell all. And believe me, there'll be a bloody lot of quaking souls when Paula tells all." She winked. "Of course, I'm willing to wager there'll be those who'll pay more pounds to keep me mouth shut than I'll make on me book!"

Jenny took note of her flashy looks—cherry-red lipstick, blue eyeshadow, heavy mascara, long, sculptured nails, a sparkling ring on every finger, gold bracelets dangling at her wrists. "Well, that's very interesting," she pleasantly told her. "I guess it would be fun working on a ship all the time, though I'd probably get tired of it."

"Not me," Paula giggled. "Too much to see and do. And I fancy meeting people, as well."

Steve self-consciously cleared his throat, then prompted,

"Tell Miss Denton what you were telling me the other day about the officers."

Jenny tensed, and felt a flash of indignant anger. She turned to glare at Steve, but he was not looking at her, had suddenly become quite interested in a rack of postcards next to the register.

Paula was only too happy to oblige, and at once leaned to confide in a mock stage whisper, "Well, it's really something, luv. You just have to be here week after week to see how those *white wolves* they're called, break so many young girls' hearts. Bleedin' shame, it is."

Jenny bit down on her lower lip, told herself to just be cool. What difference did it make what this gossipy woman had to say anyway?

Paula took a deep, excited breath, enjoying herself. "*This* story will break your heart, for sure. Heard it from the chaplain, himself. He says he got a letter from a young girl somewhere in Texas, crying to him because an officer she had a romance with a few months back hadn't answered her letters."

Jenny remained tight-lipped, but Steve gasped, "Why would she write to the *chaplain*? Didn't she realize it was just a shipboard romance? I mean, what could the chaplain do because she'd made a fool of herself?"

Giving her long red hair a toss, Paula snickered, "Now what woman wants to admit that? Remember, he'd probably made her feel like she was the only woman in the world. Those silver-tongued devils got a way of doing that. I've seen it happen time and again.

"Anyway . . ." she went on. "This poor girl wrote to the chaplain saying she just knew something *terrible* had happened to the officer. She'd tried calling the ship, but the high seas operator said she couldn't locate him on board. Now remember, this girl believed this officer, because he'd sworn he loved her and wanted to marry her.

There was just no way she was going to believe there'd be another reason she hadn't heard from him except for something awful happening to him.''

"And *had* something awful happened?'' Steve anxiously waited to hear.

Jenny gritted her teeth. Did he really believe she was so dumb she couldn't see this whole thing was staged? Maybe Paula wasn't making up the gossip she was so eagerly passing along, but, for sure, Steve had already heard it, set it up to be repeated for her sake.

Paula snickered again. "Oh, yes, something bloody well awful *had* happened! And you know what it was?'' She looked at them in turn.

Jenny stared at her frostily.

Steve urged her on. "No, tell us!''

Paula laughed, "The bloke told the chaplain he couldn't even remember *which one* she was!''

"No!'' Steve gasped.

"I swear it. The chaplain told it, himself, that when he called the officer in and started talking about getting some letters from a girl named Debbie, the officer looked straight at him, he did, and said, 'Well, sir, you'll have to be more specific. There are lots of girls named Debbie, and I just can't recall which one she was'!''

Steve shook his head in mock pity and gave an exaggerated sigh. "A sad, sad thing. Say!'' He snapped his fingers, laughed loud and heartily to make sure it was understood he was only joking before asking, "The officer's name wasn't Moen, was it?''

Paula looked surprised at that, and Jenny knew that was not part of the arrangement she'd had with Steve to repeat her story for her benefit. "Uh, no, no it wasn't,'' she was quick to assure. "Not Officer Moen. T'wasn't him a'tall.''

She began to ring up the film, and Jenny noticed she was quite nervous. Her hand shook as she finally passed the bag across the counter. "Thank you now. Have a good cruise!" she said and turned quickly to disappear behind the curtains that concealed a storage room.

Jenny waited till they were outside in the hallway, then turned on Steve with vehemence. "That was tacky, insensitive, and cruel. I don't care for my sake, because I form my own opinions of people and never pay any attention to gossip. But I feel sorry for that girl. You embarrassed her. Officer Moen happens to be Chief Officer Senior, a very high rank, and if he finds out she spreads vicious gossip about officers to passengers, she'll probably lose her job."

He was unmoved and merely shrugged off her reprimand. "Well, I thought maybe if you heard it from someone besides me, you'd believe all the stories about officers. There's a joke," he went on to inform, "that the only difference between a *one-week* cruise and a *one-night* stand is six nights."

"Very funny!" Jenny snapped.

She started to walk away, but he caught her arm, immediately contrite. "Hey, I'm sorry," he said, then rushed to bluntly confide, "If you want to know the truth, I'm jealous as hell. I saw you with that guy this afternoon, and I couldn't stand it. I *didn't* set anything up with that shopgirl, I swear it. True, I'd been in there earlier, and an officer came in with a woman, and she voluntarily started telling me what Romeos they are, how disgusting it is to everybody else on board—the cruise staff, shop girls, everybody who works on the ship. She sees it happen every week. They stand at the railing in Miami when passengers are coming on board, trying to pick out the women traveling alone, the young ones, pretty ones, and then they zero in later, in the disco, or by the pool. They give them a big time all week and the women eat it up. They've got a guy in a fancy uniform squiring them around, somebody to dance with, walk with on the decks in the moonlight, go ashore with. They've got somebody to be in love with on the *Love Boat*. Don't you see it? Then on Saturday morning, they kiss them good-bye at the gangplank, send them home with lots of beautiful memories that'll turn sour as soon as they realize it was all make-believe, a fantasy, and then the vicious cycle starts all over again when the next passengers start coming on board that afternoon.''

Jenny knew she should be indignant instead of amused, but she could not help herself, as she challenged with a saucy smile, "So what I'm hearing from you, Steve, is that you think *I'm* dumb and naive and inexperienced with men and all it takes to sweep me off my feet is a white uniform, a moon, and a cruise ship. Great! Thanks a lot! I think you're great, too!'' She threw up her hands and began to walk toward the dining room.

Steve hurried along beside her to plead his case. "No, I'm not saying that at all. I know you're extremely smart and absolutely wonderful in every way. Why do you think I'm beating my head against the wall trying to get you to notice me? Because I'm crazy about you! And all I'm asking you to do is to give me a chance to show you what a great time we can have together. You're the woman I've been looking for, Jenny, and I don't like getting beat before I even get a chance to play the game, all because this damn ship is a floating Disney World!''

Jenny laughed again. "That's *your* interpretation, not mine. Just because your fantasies aren't coming true, you think everybody else is crazy.''

"That's not so. All I'm asking for is a chance.''

She stopped walking, turned to look up at him with narrowed, thoughtful eyes, then grabbed him by his sleeve and pulled him to one side, away from the traffic and stares of passersby. "Let me tell you something, Steve. I like you. I think you're an all right kind of guy. When we get back to Atlanta, I'd like a chance to get to know you better. We can have dinner. Maybe I'll even take you up on your very *kind* offer to rent me office space, *if* we can keep it on a professional level. No strings. No favors. But right now I'm having a great time with a guy I happen to also like. A lot. And if you persist in trying to meddle in my business by playing childish pranks like setting me up to hear some gossipy shopgirl spread vicious tales, then you're going to ruin any chance of our even being friends. Have you got that?''

Like a petulant child, his lower lip dropped, along with his chin, and he stared down at his shiny black patent-leather shoes. He drew in his breath, let it out slowly, then dared to offer, ''Well I just want you to be sure you know what you're doing, and—''

''Hey!'' She grabbed his sleeve again, gave him a rough jerk, forcing him to look down at her and meet her very determined gaze. ''Read my lips, bucko! I'm a big girl!'' she said firmly.

''Okay,'' he finally grumbled, then blurted, ''But I don't mind telling you I hope you get burned by that guy, and when you do, remember I'm waiting in the wings to help you pick up the pieces and get on with your life— with *me*!''

''Steve . . .'' Jenny shook her head and sighed. ''You're all heart!''

ELEVEN

Dinner, Jenny decided by the time appetizers were served, was not going to be a very enjoyable experience that evening. Russ was wolfing down his food and seemed to be in a bad mood, speaking to no one. This made Carla nervous *because* she barely picked at her food and was jumpy and tense. Meanwhile, Steve withdrew within himself, pensive. Jenny thought the meal would never end!

Halfway through the main course, Russ glanced at his new watch and cried to no one in particular, "Hey, it's time for the casino to open!" He got up so quickly his chair nearly tipped over backward. Carla was right behind him, forgetting all about her food, which she'd hardly touched anyway.

For the first time, Steve came out of his shell. He stared after them, tearing across the dining room like the fire sirens had just sounded. "What's with them?"

"The casino just reopened," she dully told him. "According to Carla, Russ dropped a bundle this afternoon, and he's anxious to try and win it back."

"*That* . . ." he contemptuously observed, "is the true

sign of someone with a real problem. It's a shame Carla doesn't wise up. Have you tried talking to her?"

"I try to stay out of other people's business," she replied pointedly.

He frowned. "Well, if everybody thought like that, it would be a sick, sick world. You have to help those who won't help themselves."

"That makes for a thin line between helping and meddling."

He was silent for the remainder of the meal, but when Jenny declined dessert and coffee and got up to go, he quickly leaped to his feet. "Would you like to go with me to the nightclub show?" he offered. "I promise not to *meddle*," he lightly added.

She had several hours to wait before meeting Kirk, so decided why not. Maybe now that she'd expressed herself and let him know how truly annoyed she was, he'd back off a bit and they could just enjoy each other's company.

The show was a South Seas variety type, with drinks served in coconut shells. The cruise staff took the opportunity to pass out Valhalla's brochures on their regular Caribbean cruises to solicit business after the European jaunt was over. Happily dizzy with Rum punch, Jenny tossed hers aside, knowing she was ultimately going to deliver a proposal to the powers that be at Valhalla that would make them sit up and take notice—along with the rest of the cruise-loving public.

When the show was not quite over, Jenny was surprised to see Carla and Russ walk in. She waved them over, and Steve scooted over in the booth to make room. "I'm glad you're here," she whispered to Carla. "You miss a lot hanging out in that casino."

"You lose a lot, too," Carla quipped, glancing worriedly at Russ before leaning to confide, "He lost all his cash, and they don't take credit cards."

"Good," Jenny bluntly declared. "Maybe he's learned his lesson, and now you can enjoy the rest of the cruise."

Carla looked doubtful, and made no further comment. They settled in to watch the show, but Jenny noticed she was not really having a good time.

When the show ended, Steve suggested they stay for dancing. Jenny figured she could spare a little time. But, after being on the floor for three straight songs, she began to fret about being able to get away. Then, seeing how miserable Carla was, and with Russ in such a foul mood, she hit on an idea and leaned over and whispered to Steve, "How about asking Carla to dance? I'll ask Russ. Maybe we can cheer them both up."

"Good idea," he agreed, liking the idea. He felt it made them more of a couple. He also was willing to do anything to get back in her good graces after the scene before dinner. But he was not giving up. He'd stop at nothing to prove to her he was the right guy for her. He'd just have to move a bit slower, be a bit more subtle, not come on like a freight train. The most important thing he'd learned about Jenny Denton was that she truly had a mind of her own, was not intimidated or easily led. "We'll dance a little while, get them in a good mood, then go to the midnight buffet," he offered. "Then, if you like, we can go to your suite, and we can all have a nice chat. We can plan our shore excursion tomorrow, get Russ's mind off gambling, and—"

Already, Jenny was walking off the dance floor and heading for the booth. She was not about to make any commitments for the rest of the evening, much less for the next day. One dance with Russ, and she was *out of here* . . . to go where she wanted to go, be with the person she wanted to be with!

Steve was right behind her and did not give Carla a chance to refuse as he grabbed her and whisked her onto the floor. Jenny had sat down, not about to be so eager with Russ, especially when she could hardly stand him. She decided to finish her drink, then make her magnanimous offer, but just then the waiter appeared to ask if they wanted another round.

"Nothing for me," Russ said, getting to his feet and curtly walking out.

Jenny stared after him, then looked up at the waiter. "No, no." She shook her head, looking beyond him to where Steve and Carla were dancing on the opposite side of the floor. She reached for the tab on the tray and quickly signed it, adding a generous tip. "That'll take care of what we've all had so far." Then she got up and hurried out before the music ended. Steve could get angry if he wanted to. Time had slipped by and it was well after midnight. She had to go and change, for she was not about to leave Kirk's cabin in the morning wearing her formal gown, and he was, no doubt, already there and wondering where she was.

Kirk sat on the sofa, nursing a white wine. He had been disappointed not to find Jenny there waiting for him. She was obviously somewhere having a good time. But after all, he was the one working. *She* was on vacation. He had to sandwich in time to be with her and was exhausted trying to hold down his job at the same time. But Jenny Denton was above and beyond anyone he'd ever met. He didn't care if he turned into a walking zombie by the time they got back to Amsterdam. He wanted to spend every possible moment he wasn't working with her and he intended to do just that.

He glanced at the time. Nearly half past twelve. He'd showered and put on his day uniform. If she didn't show up soon, he was going to change into evening attire and go look for her. There had been a few occasions in the past when he'd struck up a relationship with a girl early on in the cruise, only to have her dump him for some wealthy guy she figured she could hang on to back in the States.

Stop it! He shook his head to clear away such negative thoughts. She wasn't like the others. There was just something about her, something he could not quite put his finger on, that told him she was different. Maybe it was because she'd been burned, too. And she would know what it was like to be hurt, would never do it on purpose. Yet they'd make no promises to each other, and he could not be really sure how she felt about him.

Before the dinner party in Oslo when they'd be around the CEO's of the company, he'd need to tell her of his real connections with Valhalla. It wouldn't do for her to find out on her own. She'd wonder why he hadn't told her, and how could he say, *"Because I wanted to make sure you weren't like the others? that you really cared about me?"* She might not understand, might think he'd been leading her on, playing games. They would be in Oslo for two days. The first day he planned to show her around the city and then he'd find the right time and place for telling her everything.

He heard the sound of a key in the door and got to his feet.

Jenny saw him and stepped in quickly to cry, "I'm late! I couldn't get away. Did you miss me?"

"Miss you?" He stepped from behind the coffee table to gather her in his arms and rain kisses all over her face. "I've thought of nothing else since I left you. Seeing you in that ballroom, glamorous as a movie star, and sitting with someone else didn't exactly help the situation," he added, holding her away from him to flash an accusing glare.

"You don't have to worry about Steve," she said, laying her head on his chest and reveling in his nearness, his warmth, the masculine smell of him. "You don't have anybody to worry about, Kirk. You're stuck with me . . . at least till the cruise is over."

"Maybe I won't let it end," he laughed, cupping her chin and raising her lips for his kiss. "Maybe I'll whisk you away to an island somewhere, make you my love slave for the rest of your life. We'll go naked and live on coconuts and pineapples, and we'll raise a family, all in a grass hut."

"Coconuts and pineapples will get old," she warned. "The rest of it—going naked, raising a family, living in a grass hut—*that* I can handle, but once in a while I've got to have pizza and a Big Mac."

"Women!" He rolled his eyes, and released her. "Always thinking about food."

"Hey!" She snapped her fingers. "Speaking of my favorite subject—"

"Midnight buffet means I've got to change," he reminded in a tone of voice that revealed he really wasn't crazy about that idea, "but we can get a sandwich in the officers' galley. That is," he added jovially, "if you like Norwegian food—smoked salmon, cold fish sticks, and brown cheese. That's usually all that's available this time of night."

"Sounds great," she said enthusiastically.

They left the cabin and walked down the narrow corridor to a door marked Galley into a world of stainless steel. Kirk opened a refrigerator door and brought out a tray of assorted cold meat, sliced tomatoes, and lettuce. He directed Jenny to a cabinet for bread. "I have Cokes in my cabin," he said, balancing two plates and nodding toward the door.

They made their way back, and after placing the food on the coffee table, he took two frosty cans of Coke from the little refrigerator beneath the wet bar, then sat down beside her.

As they ate, their conversation was general, but afterward, settling back against the sofa, Kirk suddenly asked, "Tell me. Just who *is* Jenny Denton from Atlanta?"

"What a question!" she laughed, then confided, "I guess I'm still trying to find that out, and in a way, maybe I hope I never do."

He raised an eyebrow. "I don't understand."

She shrugged, and also settled back. "I don't know. You read so many articles these days about finding yourself and learning to like yourself. It's supposed to be trendy to be able to say, 'I feel *good* about myself.' Well, I *do* feel that way, but I also like the feeling that there's still more for me to learn about myself. I don't like the idea that this is it. This is *me*."

"That I can relate to. I meet so many people in this job, and their comments are always the same: 'You're so lucky to be on a cruise ship all the time.' I don't share their feelings, because I'm starting to think there's no challenge, nothing new to be learned—about me, or my life."

She found that surprising. "I have to agree with everyone else. I think I'd like being on a cruise all the time. It would be a bit hedonistic to be sure," she admitted with a grin, "but nice just the same."

"It gets boring. Week after week. Same ports. Same sights. This particular cruise to my own country is a welcome change, but also a rarity."

"Then you don't like sailing?" she asked incredulously. "But I thought all sailors sailed because they love the sea."

He laughed softly. "I take it you believe Masefield's poem—'I must go down to the seas again, to the lonely sea and the sky. And all I ask is a tall ship and a star to steer her by . . .' "

She nodded and finished the verse, " 'And the wheel's kick and the wind's song and the white sail's shaking, And a gray mist on the sea's face and a gray dawn breaking . . .' Sounds wonderful to me . . . You read a lot of poetry, don't you?" she suddenly pointed out.

"And so do you. Seems we have a lot in common."

She was drowning in those incredible blue eyes again, and the tremors within had begun. She had to force herself to keep talking. "But if you don't like your job, why do you keep doing it?"

"I didn't say I was unhappy. I just said that it's not the fantasy, the paradise, you and everyone else makes it out to be. It gets lonely. I think about a home to go to when I get off work, instead of a cabin with a porthole. I think about relationships that last longer than a week at a time."

Jenny could not help wondering just how many of those week-long romances he'd had. "But you were married," she reminded. "You still have a home in Bergen."

"Have you ever been married?" he asked.

She shook her head.

"Do you think you'd like to be married to a sailor?"

"Is this a proposal?" she could not help quipping.

"Not yet," he bantered right back. "But you never know. You're a beautiful woman."

"Well, thanks," she was able to murmur, then pointed out, "But beautiful women don't always make beautiful wives."

"True. And getting back to what you said—yes, I was married, but it didn't work out."

"I'm sorry," Jenny offered.

"I'm not. We got married too young and we were never that happy. I didn't realize it at the time. I think I believed marriage was supposed to be that way, that the passion and thrills wear off after a while. Now I feel differently.

I don't think it has to be that way, not if two people work at it. My ex-wife and I obviously didn't.

"But why haven't *you* ever married?" he suddenly, bluntly asked. "Was your last experience the only time you've ever been engaged, or come close to it?"

"No, there were a few others," she lamented, then said, "I guess the truth is that I've concentrated on my career instead of my personal life."

"Maybe it's time we changed all that. For both of us."

His eyes burned into hers with passionate longing, and his lips brushed against hers warmly. She yielded, melting against him, helplessly succumbing to the wildy pulsating feelings coursing recklessly through her veins.

Once again they were lost in each other. This time, he did not carry her to the bed; instead, he pushed away the coffee table so they could roll easily to the carpet.

In near frenzy, they tore off their clothes, and when they were naked, neither wanted foreplay. Both were trembling with eagerness. "Now . . ." Jenny urged. "Take me now, please . . ."

"Never before," he murmured hotly, more to himself than her as he finally answered her pleas and maneuvered on top of her writhing body, "never ever before have I wanted anyone more . . ."

She lifted her legs to wrap them around his strong back, her neck arching backward as he thrust himself inside her, filling her, and she gasped in wonder. Almost at once, she was ravished by an ecstatic climax, then realized in wonder that the feeling was not ending. He was taking her up once more, for he knew how to move within her to touch a heretofore undiscovered realm of joy. She felt the wonder building again, higher, higher, and cried out loud as the overwhelming zenith began to explode.

He smothered her sounds of rapture with his lips, devouring her in a kiss that rocked them in unison with his undulating hips. She felt his own release in hard, pummeling jabs that served only to intensify her own volcanic peak. Yet he did not stop, but moved onward and onward, as though he could not bear to bring himself to finality. Jenny frantically wondered if it would ever end, realized she did not want it to, would ride joyfully with him as long as the wings of rapture carried them onward.

At long last he slowed, and, still inside her, gently rolled her to one side and held her tightly against him. He gazed at her adoringly, brushed her hair lovingly back from her face. For a while, neither spoke, lost in the magic of the moment. Finally, he took a deep, ragged breath and firmly avowed, "Never like this, Jenny. Never has it been like this. You're everything a man could want . . . and more. And I don't ever intend to let you go."

She cradled her head against his shoulder, sleepily wondering if it was all real and not just a dream, a part of the fantasy world of cruise ships.

─────────── TWELVE ───────────

The S.S. *Misty Seas* dropped anchor at the northernmost point of Europe, where the land was bathed in a constant ethereal light, for the sun would not drop below the horizon for seventy-nine consecutive days.

Jenny knew that if she were not already in love with Kirk, she was coming dangerously close to it. And what then? He might be drawn to her, feel something akin to love, but *did* he love her? And what of the other women in his life? They had not talked of them, and she could not help wondering if there were any . . . or how many. There was no denying he was irresistibly handsome, and, for sure, any woman he made love to would never be able to forget him. He sailed week after week on the *Misty Seas'* regular itinerary—romantic Nassau, beautiful San Juan, tropical St. Thomas, and mystical St. Maarten. By day he was in a world of bikini-clad women, voluptuous bodies slick with coconut oil, sipping tropical rum and pineapple drinks. By night the mood became one of champagne, soft music, and moonlight. How could he resist one affair after the other? And, she could not help fretting, that might be all she was to him—another fling, another encounter along the way. And Jenny knew she could not deny her fears any more than she could deny how each time they were together, she cared even more for him.

As they were boarding the bus after the tour to return to the ship, a matronly woman approached Kirk. "You Norwegians have such a beautiful, beautiful country," she commented amiably. "Yet I understand there are more of you living in America now than live in Norway. I can't understand why." She smiled, shook her head, and went on her way.

Jenny and Kirk were standing a bit back from the others, and suddenly he squeezed her hand. She looked up at him as he solemnly confided, "Maybe they found something there that was more important than their native country. Maybe they found the person they wanted to spend the rest of their lives with."

Jenny once again thought she would surely drown in the intensity of those tropical eyes. She swallowed hard, swayed and fought to keep her voice controlled as she said, "Maybe that person would be willing to live in *your* world."

"Maybe . . ." there was the play of a smile on his lips, "two people could find the best of both worlds . . . *together*."

She wanted to kiss him then and there, knew he wanted that, too. From below she could hear the savage crashing of the waves against the rocks as the same wild intensity seemed to lap over her entire body in heated ripples of desire.

He shook his head ever so slightly, as though in wonder as he murmured, "My God, Jenny, I've never felt this way before. I swear to you. At no other time in my life have I felt such a peace when, at the same time, a hurricane rages inside me. I know we only just met, but it's like I've known you always and ever, that we lived before, loved before, in another world, another time, and I know it's only because you have always been alive for me, in my heart—the one woman I was dreaming of, living for, searching for. I don't think I can let you go.''

''I don't think I want you to. It's just that—'' How could she explain to him the fierce turmoil within when she did not understand it herself? ''Things . . .'' she began hesitantly, ''are happening fast, Kirk, maybe too fast for me to grasp the meaning of it all.''

He looked down at her in confusion as he tried to comprehend her meaning. ''What is there to grasp? We care about each other. Deeply. No matter that it *has* happened fast. Whoever said there was a time limit on knowing in your heart how much you care for someone?''

Jenny was angry with herself, for how could she tell him that she was starting to feel insecure, fearing deep inside that just maybe he was just putting her on? That he might be lying about his feelings for her just to keep her in his bed every night till this cruise ended and he could pick up a new ''officer groupie'' on the next? Did she really want him to think she was that uncertain—about him, herself . . . life and love and romance? *No!*

''Jenny . . .'' He placed his hands on her shoulders, and gave her a gentle shake. It didn't matter that everyone was on the bus waiting for them to board. Nor did it matter that it was a staunch rule that an officer involved romantically with a female passenger was not to be demonstrative in public in any way. Kirk only knew that he could feel doubt in Jenny, unhappiness, and he did not like it. ''Jenny, I've told you that I never cared for anyone the way I care for you, and it doesn't matter whether we've only been together a few days, a few weeks—or years. I only know that the more we're together and the more I know you, the more I care about you."

"I feel the same way," she was quick to assure him. "It's never been this way for me, either, and it just seems unreal because it's all happened so fast. We are, after all, living a fantasy, Kirk. At least I feel like *I* am."

His fingers pressed hers gently, and he was almost trembling with desire to kiss her then and there. "Don't question fate, Jenny, not when it's good to you."

"Hey," the driver called, impatiently, "unless you two want to walk back to the ship, let's go."

"I don't know about walking," Kirk laughed down at her, "but right now, I think I could fly."

"Me, too," she happily agreed, yearning to be in his arms, willing them to be able to soar up and above the clouds, to transport themselves instantly back to the solitude of his cabin.

He began to lead her toward the waiting bus. "We've lots of time to talk about how dreams can, and do, come true, my dear."

Due to its size, the ship was anchored out a ways, and it was necessary for passengers to be transported by one of the two tenders. While waiting to board the next outgoing tender, Kirk excused himself, saying he needed to make a phone call to Bergen and it was cheaper to do so from shore than from ship. He left her at the waiting point and said he would return shortly.

Jenny wandered to the window of a nearby store to admire little souvenir trolls. Kirk had said to wait till they got to Oslo to buy anything, for prices were much higher on Mageroya.

Suddenly she glanced up at the reflection in the plate glass and gasped in surprise. Steve was standing right behind her. She whirled around. "Hi," she greeted him. "I didn't hear you come up."

"I'm surprised you even recognize me," he said tonelessly. "Remember me? The guy who's mad about you?"

She forced a laugh, not really liking his attitude. "Sure, the one with the kind face! How'd you like the North Cape?" She wanted to get the conversation turned from a personal level.

Wistfully, he murmured, "Well, it would've been more fun with you. You really turned into Cinderella last night, you know, disappearing at the stroke of twelve."

Jenny did not know what had happened after she left, for when she'd returned to the cabin that morning after spending the night in Kirk's, Carla was not around to fill her in. "Well, were you able to show Carla a good time?" she asked, breezily. "Russ left before I did."

"Oh, we walked around for a while, looking for both of you. We didn't find you, of course," he said with a touch of bitterness, "but Russ was in the casino. With an older woman who gave him a stake. He lost that, too," he added wryly.

She raised an eyebrow, thought how torn Carla must be.

Suddenly, sharply, he reached to clasp her hand and ask, almost in desperation, "I'd like to have you all to myself tonight, Jenny. Let's make it a wonderful evening. Dinner. Dancing. A show in the lounge. A walk on deck in this wonderful, strange light. How about it? The clock is ticking, and I want a chance to show you *we* can have a good time together, too."

She hated to hurt him or anyone else, but good grief! She had never encountered someone so persistent. "It's just that—"

"It's just that everybody has to have somebody on the *Love Boat*," he cut her off with a slight sneer and a wry smile, "and your officer found you before I did. But I promise you one thing—I don't give up easily, and I'm waiting in the wings, so he'd better be good to you." He turned and walked away, shoulders slumped.

Jenny stared after him, shaking her head, and was glad to see Kirk approach.

On the short ride back to the ship, Jenny concentrated on the dazzling scenery. Snowcapped mountains in the distance and the dazzling waters of the sea were breathtaking to behold in the ethereal light of the never-ending day.

Happily, Jenny exulted to Kirk, "I'm having such a good time seeing the beauty of Norway that I wonder how I'll be able to prepare a brochure on the Caribbean. I'll never be able to get this cruise out of my mind."

"I hope not, but don't worry," he quickly offered, "you'll have a Caribbean cruise to write about. After my vacation and I'm back on for the regular runs, you can come back on board as my guest."

"Your guest?" she echoed, not understanding.

"Well, you'll remember I told you officers have a tour of duty for four straight months, then they're off for two. On each tour, we're allowed to have a guest for two one-week cruises. That's so officers who are married can have their wives on board. But single officers can have guests, too, so I thought maybe you'd like a vacation in the Caribbean this fall."

She was overwhelmed and said as much.

"I have an ulterior motive," he warned with a mock leer and a mischievous gleam in his eye.

"No problem there," she cracked, good-naturedly, following his provocative lead.

"*That's* not what I'm talking about. I'm going to try to maneuver you into inviting me to visit you in Atlanta when I go on vacation after dry-docking in Hamburg."

"I thought that was already understood!"

He winked. "I was just testing, to see if you remembered and really meant it."

"Of course, I do, and you . . ." she gave him a playful poke in the chest with her forefinger, "better not forget you invited me to come back to Norway as your guest, if I can work it out with the tough schedule I'll have when I get back home," she added thoughtfully.

When they stepped off the tender and walked up the gangplank into the entry hold on C deck, a stern-faced officer signaled to Kirk. He left Jenny standing to one side as he hurried over, and she watched his brow furrow as he listened. Then he returned to explain he had to report for duty at once. They began to walk through the narrow corridor, toward a crew elevator, which Kirk preferred to use. Quickening her pace, because he seemed in a hurry, she asked, "Is something wrong?"

He glanced over his shoulder to make sure no one could overhear, then told her a passenger, an elderly woman, had died. The ship's doctor judged the cause to be a heart attack. Her body had to be taken to the morgue, and it was part of his duties as Chief Officer Senior to handle all the paperwork and legal procedures.

"That's awful," Jenny said, remembering that he'd told her earlier that it was not so uncommon for elderly passengers to die on a cruise. She felt tremendous sorrow for the woman's traveling companions, and she asked about them.

"Well, if this were our regular run in the Caribbean, the body would just remain in the morgue till we got back to Miami, but because we still have over a week left on this cruise they don't want to continue. They want to fly with her body back to the States, but that isn't possible till we reach Oslo. No major airports till then."

They got on the elevator with two other crewmen, and nothing more was said till they reached Kirk's deck. She stepped off with him though she did not intend to go to his quarters with him since he was in a hurry. "Rest up," he softly said to her. "Have dinner. Go to one of the shows and have a good time. Then, later . . ." his husky voice trailed meaningfully, "make yourself at home in my cabin, if you feel like it . . ."

"I already do feel like it," she whispered tremulously.

He glanced around, saw they were not alone as passengers made their way to their cabins, so he blew her a kiss, caressed her with a warm smile, and continued on his way.

When Jenny got back to the Venus suite, the telephone was ringing, and she smiled to think maybe Kirk was calling to say he missed her or some such flirting banter.

"Hi, there . . ." she answered brightly.

It was not Kirk. Instead, she heard an unfamiliar male voice crisply inquire, "Miss Sutton?"

"No. This is her cabinmate. Carla isn't here right now. May I take a message?"

"Yes, please. This is the purser's office. Just tell her that her request for a cash advance on her Optima card has been approved. She can pick it up before nine o'clock tonight. We close then."

Jenny said she would tell her and hung up the phone. Cash advance? Why would Carla need cash? Everyone on board took credit cards, and so did the souvenir shops in port.

Strange, she mused, then pushed the thought aside as she began to undress to take a shower. Dress for the evening, she recalled, was again casual. Formal nights were mostly scheduled for the evenings when they were at sea, and passengers would not be busy settling in after coming back onboard and—

Cash advance!

Jenny was suddenly positive she knew why Carla needed cash!

She was also sure her jolting revelation could only mean trouble for her foolish friend.

There was, she remembered, only *one* place on the ship that refused to take credit cards.

The casino!

The S.S. *Misty Seas* sailed on into the fjords of Norway, and Kirk was with Jenny every possible moment he was not on duty. Sharing her delight in the wonders of his country was like taking a wonderstruck child to her first circus. Through her eyes he saw the beauty he had always taken for granted.

In Andalsnes, a small charming village on the Romsdals fjord, high mountains with jagged peaks surrounded them. Jenny, struck by the awesome landscape, told Kirk that she had read there were eighty-seven snowcapped peaks. Kirk teased that there were once eighty-*eight* but that American tourists chipped away souvenirs till there was nothing left.

She laughed with him, loving his sense of humor. Never could she remember having so much fun with anyone. They had, she was sure, the best of everything—passion, good times together—all a woman could ask for in a man.

In Trondheim they walked, hand in hand, the narrow, twisting medieval streets still existing from the tenth century. They stopped at the main square, a vast, open space equipped for traffic, parking, newsstands, flower stalls, and an outdoor market. That day, in honor of the ship being in port with so many American passengers, the Stars and Stripes snapped in the breeze everywhere they looked. And, despite having such a wonderful time, Jenny got a lump in her throat as she looked at the flags.

Kirk noticed her mood, and when he asked if she were homesick she had to admit she was. "All you need is some junk food to snap out of it," he laughed. "I'll see if I can find a place."

"Fine," she quipped in turn. "Just make sure you don't find one of my old accounts!"

Kirk wanted to show her the great Nidaros Cathedral, Trondheim's pride. Built in the Middle Ages, Christians from all over Europe made pilgrimages to it. "I warn you, though," he said in a mock serious whisper, "it's haunted by the ghost of a monk, and it is said that anyone with a deceitful heart will feel his wrath if they dare enter."

Jenny knew he did not really believe the legend but she went along with it. "And what does he consider a deceitful heart?"

They were standing together on a thickly tree-shaded sidewalk bordered by a draping chain fence that ran the length of the grassy strip along the massive structure. No one else was around at that moment and suddenly Kirk gathered her in his arms to hold her so close she could feel the warmth of his breath upon her face. As she looked up at him, there was something strangely discerning in his gaze. "When a man is in my kind of situation, Jen . . ." he began, "he meets all kinds of people, all kinds of women. When I first went to work for the cruise line, I had to learn a lot. Women, in general, can be hard to figure out, but when you are a foreigner trying to figure out an *American* woman, well . . ." He paused to give a wry smile, then continued. "What I'm trying to say is that I've been fooled a few times by misguided intentions. Some women live in fantasyland—"

"I've thought of that term often in the past week," Jenny quietly interjected.

"Well, what I am trying to say is that some women come on a cruise and *live* their fantasies, then they return to the real world. I only hope what we've shared won't just be part of your fantasies, that I will be a part of your real world."

She stood on tiptoe to kiss him, and then they clung together for long, steaming moments when both wished they were not in a churchyard but back on the ship, in his cabin, answering the wild, savage hunger that coursed through their bodies.

At last she tore herself from him, and, attempting to lighten the sensual mood, grinned up at him impishly to urge, "Come on, my Viking lover. Let's go into that cathedral and see if your ghost hits me over the head with his chains!"

They walked inside, where the air smelled of candle wax and incense. It was hushed, quiet, with only a few people kneeling at the altar in meditation and prayer. Jenny walked around to admire the magnificent stained glass and icons for a time.

Outside once more in the brilliant light of day, Jenny said, "You see? We didn't hear from your old monk. That means I'm a gal you can trust!"

Suddenly, the draping chain fence behind them that separated sidewalk from grass, gave a loud, eerie rattle. "Uh-oh!" Kirk cried.

Jenny saw the twinkle in his eye, looked down to see how he had raised his leg backward to give the chain a quick shake with his toe. "Oh, you think you're cute, don't you?" she said with pretended indignity. "Well, what about *your* deceitful heart? I'll bet an American ghost would rattle chains over you!'' They laughed together and were soon locked in yet another torrid embrace.

Later, Jenny pondered the conversation, wondering all the more about Kirk's past romances. There was so much she did not know about him. They talked. Oh, yes, they talked for hours on end. He, about his country; she, about hers. He seemed to shy away from the past, however, saying it was no more than a wave crashing on the shore, dissolving into frothy bits of memory that meant nothing to the endless waves that follow.

And he asked few questions about *her* yesterdays, and it did bother her somewhat that he was not the least bit curious about, or jealous over, her private life back in Atlanta. He seemed to enjoy hearing her talk about her work, thought it interesting, challenging.

Other than that, it was as though no life had existed before the idyllic cruise, and they made tentative plans for what might happen after it was over.

So Jenny had her thrills and ecstasy, along with her doubts and fears. She had given more of herself to Kirk in a short period of time than she had ever given to any past relationship. And sometimes, when she lay curled in his arms after a torrid session of lovemaking, and they whispered to each other how much they cared, a cold chill would move up and down her spine at the tormented thought of what might happen if she found out he was not as he represented himself.

Slow down, she commanded her heart, and her heart merely laughed, *No way! No way!* And constantly she was plagued with the poignant line of another beloved poem—''seize the pleasures of the present day . . . live while you live . . .''

Did she dare savor all the present had to offer and just take one day at a time where Kirk was concerned? It was a question that plagued her more and more as the days and nights passed, and the remainder of the cruise wound down to single-digit days.

Otherwise, it was a happy time, shadowed only by her concern for Carla. Jenny slept with Kirk every night but always left his cabin as he reported for his duty. Carla was never there so she knew she was sleeping with Russ. Never at breakfast, seldom at lunch, their encounters even in the suite became fewer and fewer. It was as though, Jenny suspiciously mused, Carla did not *want* to be around her.

At dinner, Carla was far from the bubbling girl who had boarded the ship in Amsterdam. Very solicitous of Russ, she seemed tense, nervous, as though afraid to offend him. They withdrew from the others, leaving Jenny and Steve to their own conversations.

Steve, meanwhile, made it clear he had no intentions of giving up on her. He was constantly badgering her to make future dates when they got back to Atlanta, to ensure they would be "friends" and seeing each other. "Barry Manilow is going to be at the Fox in August. I'll see if I can get tickets . . ." or, "I've got a special invitation to a Falcons pre-season bash. You'll enjoy going to that."

It was, Jenny fumed, as though he was positive that once the cruise was over, so was her relationship with Kirk, and he would have a clear field. She made neither comments nor commitments, continuing to hedge.

Kirk was excited about the last two ports of call on the cruise—two days in Oslo, Norway's largest city and also the capital, and then the Briksdal glacier, unequaled in continental Europe.

The morning they were to arrive in Oslo, Kirk had the bridge call his cabin at five A.M. for wake-up. Jenny heard the excitement in his voice as he spoke in Norwegian on the phone, groggily wondered why he was so enthusiastic, then remembered they were coming into Oslo.

He bounded out of bed at once, exulting that they were going to have one of the best days yet. "And I'm taking you up on the bridge with me, because the view coming in is really something. The Oslofjord is sixty miles long!"

"That sounds fine, but . . ." She sat up quickly to protest, "You didn't say anything about that last night, and I sure can't go up on the bridge wearing *that*!" She nodded to the white silk gown lying across a nearby chair. Dinner the night before had been formal, and she had dressed accordingly. "I need time to go change."

He came back to the bed to lean over and plant a kiss on her forehead and tease, "Well, you should have thought of that, my little minx, when you attacked me the minute I came in last night! Look at your clothes, anyway, strewn all over my cabin. I can't help it if you're a nympho and can't wait to get naked!"

He retreated as she threw a pillow at him and laughingly called over his shoulder, "Meet me back here in forty-five minutes. I'll check in at the bridge, see how the schedule is running, then get us some coffee and pastry."

"Skip the pastry for me," she yelled back. "I bet I've gained five pounds on this cruise!"

"Great!" he countered. "American women are too skinny, anyway!"

She let herself out of his cabin happily, locking the door behind her with his key, then hurried on her way.

Entering the Venus suite, she heard water running in the bathroom, saw Carla's clothes strewn across her still-made bed. So, she was there for a change, Jenny thought as she went to the closet, laid out a yellow cotton jumpsuit, nylon windbreaker, Nikes—an outfit meant for a long day of sightseeing and all the walking that went with it.

She began to remove her makeup with cold cream, then, as she reached to throw the solid tissue in the wastebasket, saw a half-crumpled piece of paper in the bottom. She dismissed it till the casino logo leaped out at her, then could not resist taking it out for scrutiny. It was a receipt for one thousand dollars in chips.

Just then Carla came out of the bathroom, wearing her robe and towel-drying her hair. She stopped short at the sight of Jenny staring down at the casino receipt and at once snatched it from her hand. "That's . . . that's none of your business!" she stammered, her voice wavering on the verge of tears. "You have no right to snoop in my things!"

Jenny nodded adamantly. "You're right. I don't. And I wish I hadn't seen it." Then, unable to keep still any longer, said with quiet reproach, "You're paying the tab, aren't you? All of it—his clothes, the watch, and now, his gambling. That's why you got the cash advance on your credit card, isn't it?"

Carla turned away, rubbing at her hair, so furiously that Jenny was surprised it did not come out in hanks.

"He's going to pay me back, not that I should have to justify anything to *you*. Russ has plenty of money. He just didn't bring much with him, didn't know he'd meet me, and we'd be spending so much buying stuff for souvenirs of our time together, partying, champagne, stuff like that."

"Why didn't he bring a credit card like *you* did? And everybody else?"

"He doesn't believe in credit cards."

"Obviously, he believes in *yours*."

Carla threw the towel across the room and turned to glare at Jenny, hands on her hips, legs apart in a defensive stance, ready for verbal combat. "Like I said, it's none of your damn business, Jenny. You don't even know me or anything about me, what I've been through—"

"Or why in God's name you let a creep like Russ Claiborne take advantage of you like he's doing!" Jenny spread her hands in a gesture of pleading for understanding. "Carla, it's true, I don't really know you, but those first few days I knew I wanted to . . . wanted us to be friends. I liked you then, and I like you now, and that's why I'm finally sticking my nose in your business. I've wanted to say something for several days now. I hate to see you get hurt—"

"And who says I'm going to get hurt?" Carla challenged. "I told you, Russ will pay me back, and if he doesn't, it's *my* business."

"That's true, it is," Jenny conceded, "but I've been around more than you have. You were married for the past ten years, and you weren't out there in that jungle where guys like Russ are a dime a dozen. He's *using* you, and you're too blind and stubborn to see it."

"That's not so. He loves me. I know he does."

"Because he says so?"

"Right!" She gave her wet, stringy hair a defiant toss and lifted her chin. "He loves me, and he's going home with me to Chicago. We're going to live together for a while, see how it works out. Then we're going to be married. And I know what you're thinking—that I'm on the rebound, but that's not true. I can look back now and see where I messed up with Robbie, and I learned from that experience. I know what it takes to hang on to a guy like Russ."

Jenny nodded, could not resist the stinging pointer, "Yes, I guess you do—a good credit card!"

Carla grabbed up her clothes, began to dress hastily as she cried, "I don't have to listen to this, and I'm not going to. And who are *you* to give *me* advice, anyway? You're sleeping with that officer you picked up! He's probably married and has ten kids, and you're just one of his cruise groupies he meets every Saturday in Miami. So what gives you the right to sit in judgment of me?"

Very much in control, Jenny addressed only her latter contention. "I'm not sitting in judgment, Carla. Not of *you*. I'm only saying I think he's taking you for a ride. And I truly hope I'm wrong, for your sake."

Carla's clothes were disheveled, but she had managed to get them on despite her fury. Her hair was hanging wet around her face, and, void of makeup, weary from lack of sleep, Jenny thought she looked a fright. She hated to see her go out like that and did not want her to be angry.

As Carla snatched up her bag, headed for the door, Jenny moved to block her path. "Please," she begged. "Don't be angry with me. I just care what happens to you."

Dear Lord, she did not want to alienate her. She was confident the poor girl was going to need a friend; Jenny wanted to impress upon her that was exactly what she was, and not a cynical busybody.

"Please," she persisted. "I promise not to interfere or voice my opinion again. Just remember I'm here for you if you need me, okay?"

She could feel some of Carla's anger begin to leave her.

"Come on." Jenny gave her a hug, which was not returned, then offered, "I've got to meet Kirk pretty soon, but if you'll call down for coffee while I hop in the shower, maybe we can catch up on things. I don't even know what you've been doing lately."

Carla relented with a sigh. "Okay. I *do* like you, too, Jenny, and I really want us to be friends. You're wrong about Russ, and you'll see that one day."

"I hope I do." Jenny impulsively kissed her cheek, hugged her again, and this time the embrace was returned.

Carla laid aside her purse, called for coffee, then resumed drying her hair.

Jenny went to shower, all the while hoping, praying, that she would eventually be proved wrong about Russ

Claiborne—for Carla's sake—but sadly feared that was not likely to happen.

Gathering her things, Jenny groaned to realize she needed another roll of film and thought how it was going to cost a small fortune to develop all the pictures she'd taken, anyway. So what? A few more wouldn't matter. She remembered the gift shop was open only for an hour that morning and would be shutting down for the rest of the day since they were in port. Calling, " 'Bye, see you later," to Carla, she hurried out.

She had not been to the gift shop since that night Steve had introduced her to Paula Streeter and was disappointed to realize the English girl was the only clerk on duty. Maybe, she hoped, handing over her purchase to be rung up, she would not remember her.

No such luck!

Paula's eyes grew wide, and, at once, she seemed nervous. Timorously, she asked, "Say, you're the one who was in here the other night talking about officers, right? With the handsome gent? That Mr. Gentry?"

"No," Jenny was quick to stiffly correct. "*You* were the one talking about officers. Not me."

Her cheeks paled. "Hey, listen, luv. I want to apologize. I'm afraid I have a big mouth. I shouldn't have said all those things. I had no right, and—"

"No problem," Jenny interrupted, not wanting to discuss it any further. But she could not resist saying, "I never pay any attention to gossip."

"But it *wasn't* gossip. It's true. Every bit of it. It's just that I had no right to repeat it."

Jenny mutely nodded, wishing she would just shut up and complete the sale so she could get out of there.

"Are you seeing Officer Moen?"

Jenny's eyes narrowed, and she gave her a "what's-it-to-you?" kind of stare.

"Hey, listen!" Paula Streeter reached to clutch her hand, really nervous then. "Please don't say anything to him, okay? I mean, I don't really care if the other officers get mad. They know that I know how they fool around, but Officer Moen, he could have me out of here with the snap of a finger, him being who he is and all, which I'm sure you're well aware of . . ." Her voice trailed.

Jenny stared at her, puzzled. "What do you mean?" she demanded.

Paula returned her stare. "You mean you didn't know he's the nephew of one of Valhalla's biggest stockholders? One of the CEO's? Why, he's only working on this ship to get a feel for it so he can sit on the board one day and know what it is he's trying to run."

Jenny continued to look at her, aghast. Kirk? Heir to Valhalla? If that was true, then why hadn't he told her? What was the big secret? Why did he want her to think he was just a working guy, like the other officers? Unless . . .

And the needle of suspicion began to prickle.

Unless she was just another girl, another cruise, and he saw no reason to confide anything important . . . because it was all part of the game!

"Are you sure?" she demanded of Paula, who was watching her fearfully, bewildered by her reaction.

"Yes, yes, of course. I wouldn't make something like that up. I thought you knew. Oh, please don't say I said anything. Officer Moen must've had his own reasons for not telling you. But that gent you were with—Mr. Gentry, is it?" She rushed on without waiting for confirmation. "Actually, he didn't tell me which officer you were involved with, only that he's mad about you himself and he wanted me to help you realize how they are, the *other* officers, that is. I had no idea you were seeing Officer Moen, not till Mr. Gentry asked me if that was who I was talking about, and then I got worried, and, oh, please . . ." she begged, clutching her hand tighter, "don't say anything to him . . ."

Carefully, Jenny unwrapped Paula's clutching fingers from around her wrist. "Don't worry," she tightly assured. "He'll never know I heard it from you."

Jenny walked out, determined that she would not jump to conclusions. Kirk had to have a reason not to have confided the truth about himself. In time, she would find out that reason.

Till then, she would play the game, too.

_________ FOURTEEN _________

Sheltered by the forested hills on one side, the wooded city of Oslo was tempered by the waters of the fjord meandering up from the Skagerrak. Jenny was charmed by the rustic appeal, and Kirk rented a car to afford them transportation for her to see as much as possible.

"One of these days," he said with an adoring smile, "we're going to have to arrange for you to come over here in the winter months and I'll teach you to ski."

Jenny felt the familiar ripple of anticipation at the mention of a future together, then silently remembered what she'd learned from Paula Streeter about who Kirk really was—and wondered again why he had not told her.

When they got to the towering structure of the Holmenkollen ski jump, Jenny took one look and gasped, "Don't tell me you've been down *that*!"

"Of course," he proudly confirmed. "I once had an uncle who lived in Oslo, and when my parents visited, I'd go skiing here."

She shook her head in wonder, impressed by his daring.

After sightseeing and lunch, there was time for shopping

in downtown Oslo. Jenny picked out a troll that reminded of their first date at the folklore show. Kirk insisted on paying for it. Then he bought her a charm—a tiny replica of the *Oseberg* ship in pewter. He had the salesgirl put it on a chain, and, as he fastened it around her neck, whispered, "So you won't forget me and the wonderful times we've had together."

She was melted by the desire burning in his eyes and fervidly whispered in response, "As if I ever could . . ."

And once more, she wondered . . .

They went for a walk in the famous Vigeland park, and suddenly, on an out-of-the way path, Kirk turned to gather her in his arms as he whispered, "Have I told you lately how much you mean to me, Jenny Denton?"

"No . . ." she sighed, "and I'll never get tired of hearing it."

Kirk kissed her till they were both breathless, then pulled away. The time had come, he decided, to be completely honest with her. He'd thought of nothing else for days, would not let himself believe she was not truly sincere in her feelings for him, felt it safe, at last, to confide in her. He took a deep breath, let it out slowly, then said, "Jenny, I've got something to tell you."

Oh, really? she thought, suppressing a smile.

And he told her, as quickly, as simply, as possible.

She listened, then asked the question that had been burning inside all day. "Why did you wait to tell me till now? Why did you let me go on thinking you were just some poor working slob, instead of being heir to a fortune?" She could not mask the indignity in her tone.

"The truth is," he laughed to admit, "right now I *am* a poor working slob. My uncle intends for me to learn the cruise business from bottom deck to top deck. The summer

I was sixteen, I even worked as a busboy in the dining room.

"But maybe . . ." He became serious, his eyes searching hers for reaction, "I wanted time to find out who *you* really are, Jenny. Maybe I wanted to make sure it wouldn't make any difference to you that I'll one day be one of the owners of Valhalla Lines."

She threw back her head and laughed. "Oh, no problem, Kirk, really. I mean, do I look like the kind who tries to sleep my way from bottom deck to the top? Do you think I'd have tried to be better in bed if I'd known who you are?"

He protested, realizing she was close to anger. "You're wonderful in bed, like you are, and—" He shook his head, disgruntled with himself. "Damn it, what can I say to make you understand? I wanted you to fall in love with *me*, for my sake. I didn't want my background to have anything to do with it. To be honest, there have been other women who somehow managed to find out about my inheritance, and those relationships turned sour."

Jenny was still miffed that he'd dare compare *her* to *them*. With narrowed eyes, she looked up at him to softly demand, "And I suppose you won't have anything to do with whether I get Valhalla's PR contract?"

He sighed again. "Frankly, yes, a lot of that will be up to me," he admitted reluctantly. "I've been taking over a lot of the administrative duties lately."

"And the fact I slept with you, I don't suppose, would have any bearings on your decision."

"Absolutely not."

She shrugged, forced herself to appear nonchalant despite the roaring within. "Well, it's nice to know that if I lose out, it wasn't because I'm a lousy lay."

"Jenny Denton!" he cried, grabbing her shoulders to give her a vicious shake. "You know better than that. If you don't know by now that you're driving me crazy, well . . ." He grabbed her, kissed her again with bruising intensity, then forced himself to let her go.

They began to walk on, and Kirk asked about how her presentation was coming along. She said she had many photos of the interior of the ship, felt she could do a good job of convincing Valhalla's owners that a new image was needed.

"Are you ready for the dinner party tomorrow night?" he asked. "You're going to meet my uncle and the other CEO's. I want them to see you'll get the contract because you're good, not because of our relationship."

"They won't know about our relationship," she was quick to inform him.

He stopped walking to stare down at her and demand, "What are you talking about?"

She repeated, firmly, "They won't know about our relationship. I'm going to the dinner party alone."

"That's ridiculous." He started walking again, holding her hand and pulling her along with him. "It's expected that I escort you. No one will know we've been seeing each other."

"Then stop looking at me like you do."

"Like how?" He paused again.

"Like you want to make love to me."

"But I do."

"Well, don't look at me like that tomorrow night. Look at me, treat me as who I'm supposed to be—someone wanting the PR contract."

He smiled. "Okay. For tomorrow night, I'll be all business. You certainly know how to be when the situation calls for it. By the way, what made you want to strike out on your own, anyway?"

They continued on their way as she spoke. "Because I couldn't take any pride in what I was doing simply manipulating people into buying a product, because they saw it the way *I* presented it to be, not the way it truly *is*.''

''But isn't that what advertising is all about, anyway?'' he wanted to know. ''Convincing people to buy something?''

''Yes, and I guess there's a fine line between advertising, per se, and just plain conning people into buying something under false pretenses. *That*, I don't like. Take the cruise brochure, for instance. I want people to book on Valhalla Lines because I presented the ships to them the way they really are, so when they go on their vacation and spend their hard-earned money, they won't feel like it was wasted.

''Also,'' she rushed on, enthused, ''there's a lot of competition out there for cruise dollars these days.''

Kirk laughed. ''That's a fact. New ships are springing up like mushrooms in a warm rain. There haven't been so many vessels at sea at one time since the Spanish Armada. Twelve launched last year. Sixteen this year.''

''Exactly, and while you can look at a cruise vacation as being a world of no decisions bigger than whether to have one dessert or two, it can be quite dull and unpleasant if you choose the wrong ship. There's nothing sadder than a party-hearty couple stuck for ten days on a ship filled with octogenarians. And the same is true when you see an elegant couple board with a wardrobe of tuxedos and beaded gowns faced with a week where the dress code is baseball caps, T-shirts, and boom boxes.''

They reached the car. Kirk opened the door for her, beaming. ''I think you've hit on a great idea, and even if I weren't crazy about you, I'd pass along my endorsement to the powers that be.''

''You're a sweetheart.'' She leaned to kiss him on the cheek. ''I may even give you a commission.''

He winked. ''I'll take it out in trade.''

And she bantered right back, "Hey, I said *commission*. With what you'd charge if you were in the gigolo business, you'd clean out my portfolio!"

He reached to fasten her seat belt for her, deliberately brushing his hand across her breast as he whispered, "And you, my dear, would command the highest prices in France's most elegant bordellos!"

When they got back to the ship, Kirk reminded her that he did not have the eight-to-twelve duty that night. "Would you like to go with me to dinner in the officers' dining room? Then we can have a rare evening out. We can go to the musical review in the theater, then go dancing if you'd like."

"I'd like," she said without hesitation.

He said he would meet her in the Viking Queen ballroom at seven, and they went their separate ways.

She found Carla sitting by the window, a half-empty pitcher of martinis on the table. She looked so depressed that Jenny could not help asking what was wrong. Carla shrugged as she downed the rest of her drink. "Oh, I just think threesomes are boring, that's all."

"*Threesomes?*" Jenny echoed. "What are you talking about?" Opening her closet door, she began to push aside her clothes in scrutiny, finally chose a gold lamé blouse with matching camisole, black velvet slacks, matching pumps.

Then she realized Carla had not said anything, so she turned to look at her curiously. Her eyes were lackluster, and her lower lip was trembling as she raised the freshly poured martini to her mouth.

"Carla? Are you okay?"

"Fine. Fine." Her smile was tight, forced.

Jenny persisted, "But what did you mean about a threesome? What's wrong?"

She gave her hair a toss, pretended nonchalance. "Oh,

it's nothing, really. It's just that there's this woman— Roberta something or other, from California—and she's been making eyes at Russ. She staked him while I was waiting for my cash to come through to make him a *loan*.''

Jenny did not miss how she emphasized the word *loan*, and knew it was for her benefit.

''She's a lot older than we are—a widow,'' she went on to say, ''but she's got a lot of money and also a grand deluxe suite!''

Jenny raised an eyebrow.

''And that's where Russ is right now. Having cocktails. I was there, too, but I left.''

Jenny heard the warning bells and dared to ask, ''And you think he's interested in her?''

''Oh, no, no!'' Carla quickly disputed.

Too quickly, Jenny thought.

Carla rushed to assure her she was not jealous. ''It's nothing like that. I mean, golly, she's old enough to be Russ's *grand*mother. We're talking sixty-something here. No, it's not like that at all. At least not on Russ's part. He's just tickled to death to be hanging out in her place, because he's sick of his cabin on the bottom deck. The fumes from the engine room are pretty bad, I can vouch for that.'' She made a face, wrinkled her nose.

''So why aren't you with him now?''

''That woman!'' Another face. ''She's all over him like ants at a picnic. It's disgusting.''

''Well, Russ might not appreciate your abandoning him to her,'' Jenny said, though she really did not think so.

''I guess you're right.'' Carla tossed down the rest of her drink and got to her feet.

Jenny noticed she was swaying. ''How much have you had to drink?''

Carla shrugged. ''Enough, I guess, that I can go back

there and drag Russ out for dinner. Then I think we're going to have a little talk. With just a few days left, I want us to spend our time together enjoying the rest of the cruise without that old battle-ax horning in.''

She left, staggering a bit, and Jenny's heart went out to her once more. She was reminded of an old TV series, where the opening line was something about there being a million stories in the Naked City. She was starting to think the same about cruise ships!

When she went to the ballroom, Kirk was sitting at a table with three other officers. They were all wearing their evening uniforms—long-sleeved white coats with shoulder boards denoting rank, white shirt, pants, black tie and shoes. Resplendent and dignified, they politely stood as she approached, and Jenny could not help thinking if ever a man was born to wear a uniform, it was Kirk Moen.

Kirk made the introductions; one of the men she already knew—Lars Ingebretsen. ''I met you and your wife, Dayna,'' she instantly recalled. ''She was going to visit her parents at the North Cape.''

''Yes. She'll come on board on our next cruise,'' he said.

As they shared a bottle of champagne, the orchestra began to play, ''When I Fall in Love.'' Jenny and Kirk looked at each other and smiled a special smile, for that was the song that was playing the first night they had danced together.

Without a word spoken, for all was understood in a special, secret look that transcends between souls in harmony, they got up and walked onto the dance floor and into each other's arms.

The music was like a whisper on the nightwind, lulling them ever gently into a private paradise all their own. His eyes never left hers, and she returned his enraptured gaze with her own. They danced to the next song, and the next, and then, when the orchestra stopped playing, they realized not only that they were the last couple on the floor but that they were also the only ones in the ballroom, except for the musicians.

"I think," Kirk pointed out, "that we'd better go to dinner now."

Jenny nodded. "Two people could starve this way, you know? Just keep on dancing and dancing . . ."

"A wonderful way to die," he said, wanting to kiss her.

And she knew he did, because she wanted it, too.

She was surprised when he headed for the Athena instead of turning to the elevator that would take them down to the bottom deck and officers' mess. "We're going to the dining room?"

"The *officers'* dining room," he corrected. "It's adjacent to the passengers', but separate."

They entered through a side door she had never noticed and, at once, Jenny was impressed. The room was small but adequate, with seating for perhaps thirty or forty people. The amenities were similar to those offered the passengers—with white linen, fresh flowers on each table, hovering waiters, busboys scurrying about. Even the elaborate menu was the same, except for the offering of several Norwegian specialties.

They dined with the other officers who had been in the ballroom, and conversation was light, pleasant. Jenny thought the Norwegians a bit stiff and cold, and noted that even Kirk was not his usual ebullient self. The whole atmosphere was dignified, not loud and merry like in the main room. But she had decided that was a Norwegian trait—reticence that could sometimes be mistaken for arrogance. She did not find it offensive. There was, after all, a time and place for every mood.

When they finished, Kirk suggested a walk on deck, since the wind was not too brisk.

When they left Oslo, he explained, they would be sailing to the south of Norway and turning up the coast toward Briksdal, their last port. "I'm probably going to have to work double shifts for the next cruise," he said in a tone that revealed he did not care if he did, "to make up for all the swapping around I've done on this one. I've arranged to be off so we can go to the glacier together."

"Good!" Jenny firmly declared. "If you have to work double shifts, you won't have time to meet anyone else."

They were on the promenade deck, near the outside stairwell. Abruptly, he drew her inside the wind barrier that surrounded and held her in his arms as naturally as the bow of the ship cut through the black waters of the night. Tersely, almost angrily, he avowed, "I don't want anyone else, Jenny. I only want you. For now and always. Don't you understand that?" He searched her face in the moonlight. "Don't you realize that in these few days you've come to mean everything to me?"

"It happened so quickly," she said dizzily.

"And who can say how long it takes to know you're in love?" he challenged, his lips brushing hers. "You're all I ever want, Jenny. Believe that . . ."

Suddenly, at that particular moment in time, Jenny knew she had to ask the question that had been gradually building in importance ever since their love affair had begun. "Is there anyone else, Kirk? Anyone else who thinks you belong to them? You meet so many girls—"

He silenced her with a kiss, gentle at first, then whispered, "If there were, I can't remember now, because it just doesn't matter anymore, Jenny, now that I love you so much . . ." He claimed her mouth once more, parting her lips with his tongue to touch and probe until she returned his kiss with fervor.

It was not the answer she wanted, Jenny rationalized in that dizzy moment, but did she really think someone so devastatingly handsome had no past? Yet she was haunted by her own feelings of insecurity. After all, she had believed Bryan when he vowed to love only her, and then there were the terrible stories Steve told her, and Paula Streeter, and also the fact that he had already kept something very important from her. But *that* was resolved now, wasn't it? She understood all that, didn't she?

Her hands moved to clutch his shoulders and hold him yet closer. She could feel the strength in his embrace, his body, and as he held her there in cool silver moonlight, Jenny felt as though there had never been any kiss in her life before this, no night under the stars till now, and no thundering of emotions racing through her veins like liquid stardust ever, ever . . . till this wonderful, magic moment. And she had to let go of those terrible feelings of doubt, enjoy the present and think only of the future, and trust and believe—until he gave her reason not to.

They clung together till the sound of passengers coming down the steps from above made them spring apart.

"Come on," Jenny cried with a gasp. "Let's go to the disco and cool off a bit."

"I'd rather take you to my cabin and play Viking . . ." He gave a mock leer in the moonlight. "You know—rape, pillage, plunder!"

"Later," she promised, pulling him along, wanting one more dance with him looking so gorgeous, wanting to savor the rare evening together while there was still shipboard activity.

The disco was crowded, and the minute they walked in, Jenny knew it would be impossible to find space on the dance floor. Also, the music was Lambada, and she was not in the mood for that. She stood on tiptoe to whisper to Kirk, "Okay, let's go play Viking."

"Great!" He was holding her hand, started to turn around and leave, then hesitated as she held back.

Jenny was staring at a couple sitting close together in a booth just inside the door. The man, an officer, had his arm around the woman and was nuzzling her neck with his lips as she giggled and laughed while sipping her drink.

And, in the whirling, dazzling lights from the spinning glass ball above the dance floor, Jenny recognized that officer—Lars Ingebretsen, who had left his wife, Dayna, at the North Cape!

Jenny could not fall asleep.

She lay in Kirk's arms, her head on his chest.

Their lovemaking had been intense, almost desperate, as though, with the cruise drawing to a close, they could not get enough of each other.

Though exhausted, Jenny could not relax, for there were so many flurried thoughts dancing in her head. The enthusiasm for her new business was as fervent as ever, and she was optimistic about its success. Yet there were other things occupying her mind, like having fallen in love, which had not been on her priority list. Kirk was everything she wanted in a man—intelligent, compassionate, a gentleman. There were bonuses, as well, like the fact he was so fiercely handsome, and also his charming accent and the savoir faire associated with his rank and background.

But there were also negatives that had to be dealt with. No matter he would probably one day be quite wealthy. That had nothing to do with any worries she harbored. She could even understand him keeping that from her, wanting to make sure she cared for *him*, not the inheritance he'd one day receive. Still, she could not help wondering if that was his only secret.

And she had to admit to being bothered by his working and living on a cruise ship, with its ever-present aura of romance. He was the kind of man who appealed to women. And yes, the reputation of the officers—white wolves—concerned her, as well, especially after seeing Officer Ingebretsen in the disco with a woman other than his wife.

"Jenny, what's wrong?" Kirk began to caress her hair lovingly, and she realized he had not been asleep, either, must have heard her pensive sighs. Not about to confide her innermost fears, she replied, "Nothing. Just too keyed up to sleep, I guess."

"It *has* been exciting." He moved to kiss her forehead tenderly. "I've never been so happy."

Jenny did not respond, for suddenly, for no reason, the image of Bryan and Linda Lee flashed before her. That night, only hours before, he had told her he loved her, all the while knowing he soon would be sleeping with someone else. She shuddered with memories of the revulsion and humiliation she had felt in that moment.

Kirk sensed there *was* something wrong. He did not want to probe, and instead asked if she would like to go for a walk on deck. "It's supposed to be nice out tonight," he added.

She said she would, eager to do something to escape the suddenly tormenting memories.

They got up and quickly dressed. Down the corridor, a short hallway cut between two cabins to lead to the private deck that ran outside the officers' quarters. No one else was about, and they went to stand at the railing, arms about each other in quiet reverence of the black-and-silver cloak that descended.

A gentle breeze blew against their faces, and Jenny instinctively shivered against the chill of the night. Kirk's arm tightened about her as she marveled at the sky above. "I don't think I've ever seen so many stars. Look! The Milky Way! I've never seen it so brilliant . . . so defined."

Kirk told her that, as a seaman, he had spent much time star gazing, never ceasing to be amazed at the wonders of the universe. "Just like different cultures have grouped stars into different constellations, they've also interpreted their own private dreams in the Milky Way. For instance, the Bushmen of the Kalahari call it the Backbone of Night. To the Swedes, it's the Winter Street that leads to heaven. In the Hebrides islands, it's called Pathway of the Secret People."

"And the Vikings?" she asked with affection.

He made his tone mock-ferocious. "The Norsemen called it the Path of the Ghosts." Then he pointed to the brightest star in the heavens. "The North Star, Polaris, whichever name it's called . . . every time I look at it, I can't help wondering how many wanderers, hopelessly lost on sea or land, have waited till night came to try to figure out where they were by looking for it.

"First," he went on to explain, pointing to another constellation, "you have to find the Big Dipper, and then extend a line through the outer two stars of its ladle. Then you'll see the North Star looks like a dollop of cream that's fallen from the upside-down dipper."

"And what if the Big Dipper isn't visible?"

"You look for Cassiopeia, a constellation just to the other side of the North Star that's shaped like a *W*, or an *M*, depending on where you see it from, and when. It always looks like a butterfly to me."

Jenny looked at him with wonder. "You know a lot about the stars, don't you?"

Quietly, with just a touch of wistfulness in his voice, he told her, "I spend a lot of time alone, Jenny. So I come out here and study the sky, then read about the constellations and try to learn a bit more. It's sort of a hobby for a sailor, I guess. Look." He pointed then to a bright silvery light. "Venus."

Jenny was impressed as Kirk shared his knowledge with her. Then the wind picked up just enough to send them inside.

Snuggled back in Kirk's bed, they made love again, but this time without intensity. It was quiet and as tender as the night they had just visited. Finally, Jenny was able to sleep, pushing her doubts away, as the rising sun chased the stars.

But, like the celestial exodus, she knew slumber brought only temporary respite from the maelstrom within.

Kirk's wake-up call came a bit earlier than usual. After being off duty for twenty-four hours, he said he had much catching up to do on paperwork, for a replacement could only do so much in his absence. "Sleep a while longer," he urged Jenny, getting up to shower and dress. "I'll leave the sign on the door so the steward won't bother you, and I'll be back around twelve. We can have lunch."

"And the dinner party tonight?" she reminded. "What time do we leave for that?"

"Seven-thirty."

"Remember your promise."

He grinned. "Sure do," he recited. "The fact that you are great in bed, the fact that I adore you, will have absolutely no bearing on whether or not I recommend you get the PR contract. Tonight is strictly business. No one at that dinner party will ever suspect we're lovers."

She laughed.

"Then, when it's over," he leered at her, "I bring

you back here, where you can use your feminine wiles to convince me you should have the job."

She winked. "Sorry. Can't write on my back, sailor!"

And they laughed together, shared another embrace.

After he'd gone, Jenny knew she needed to return to her own cabin and start getting her notes together for that evening.

It was not yet six-thirty. She took the Do Not Disturb sign off the door, was locking it when she heard the door to the next cabin opening, then closing.

"Psst!" someone whispered.

Jenny looked around, was instantly jolted as she saw it was a woman fumbling with a key at the next door, and she also recognized her as the one she had seen with Officer Ingebretsen in the disco.

"Do you know anything about these locks?" she asked Jenny in frustration. "Is there a trick or something? I can't get it to work, and he told me to let myself out so he could sleep till it was time to go on duty, and . . ." Her voice trailed, as she gave a helpless shrug, offered a weak smile.

Jenny took the key from Kirk's door and shook her head apologetically. "Sorry," she managed to say. "I can't help you."

"Well, damn! It's just me, then," the woman laughed as the lock suddenly tumbled.

Jenny glanced up as she passed, saw that, indeed, the name plate beside the door read, INGEBRETSEN, L. She kept on going, did not look back, had no intentions of walking along with the woman in camaraderie. She told herself she was not condemning anybody; she just didn't want to be involved. What Lars Ingebretsen did was his business. She just wished she didn't know about it.

Back in her own suite, Jenny was surprised to find Carla in bed. She was not asleep, however, and sat up to wail, almost accusingly, "Oh, I wish I could've been sure you were going to stay out all night. Russ says the fumes from the engine room are seeping into his cabin, giving him a headache. He refuses to stay there anymore and Roberta is going to let him have the sofa in her suite. She didn't invite me to stay, too," she added glumly. "I guess she doesn't realize how things are between us."

"Probably doesn't." Jenny did not know what to say at that point. Not having met this Roberta, she didn't want to second-guess her motives. Then, remembering the size of the deluxe suites, she asked, "Don't those suites have *two* bedrooms?"

"Yeah, they do. Didn't I tell you? Roberta is traveling with a friend, and she's got a thing going with one of the other musicians."

It seemed to Jenny that everybody had something going with somebody but didn't want to put ideas into Carla's head by saying so. If Roberta was not interested in Russ that way, and was, indeed, only being friendly, well, she didn't want to insinuate anything.

She picked up the day's schedule from where it was still lying on the floor, pushed under the door the night before. At eleven o'clock, there was a special video presentation being given about all Valhalla's ships. The intent, no doubt, was to whet passenger appetites to the thought of going on another cruise before this one even ended. She needed to see that, because one of the things she planned in her presentation were videos on each ship, produced in vast numbers so that travel agencies could loan them out to prospective cruisers.

"Jenny . . ." Carla hesitantly spoke. "Can I ask you for a big favor?"

Jenny warily looked up from the schedule. "It depends."

"Are you going to be here . . . tonight?" She took a

deep breath. "I mean, do you think you'll be somewhere else till morning?"

"Carla, what are you getting at?" Jenny feared she already knew.

She twisted her hands nervously, bit her lower lip, finally plunged ahead. "I want to ask Russ to stay here tonight so he won't have to stay with Roberta. I mean, you know, time is running out, and—" Her voice trailed, and she turned her head toward the window and murmured apologetically, "But maybe I shouldn't ask. I mean, it's *your* place, too."

Jenny had her doubts about the fumes from the engine room being that bad, since the cabins on that deck were used continuously. She also had a strong suspicion that was not the reason Russ had been taken under Roberta's accommodating wing. Still, Carla was right about the clock ticking. It was now or never, and if Russ was who the poor girl wanted, so be it. "Okay," she said finally. "I guess there's no harm. Just have him out of here by eight o'clock tomorrow morning, okay?"

"Okay!" Carla got up and ran to give her a grateful hug. "I swear, you're the best friend I've ever had, Jenny. You don't know how much this means to me!"

She began to dance around, wrapping her arms about herself in delight, planning out loud for the evening ahead. "I'll talk him into leaving the casino early, and we'll come back here. I'll order champagne. A midnight snack. We'll dance and talk and look out the window at the ocean. Oh, it's going to be wonderful. I just know it is!"

Suddenly Carla stopped dancing around, sobered as she remarked, "I know you don't like Russ, Jenny, but he's the greatest, honest."

Greatest *what?* Jenny wondered cynically to herself. Out loud, she said, "I'm happy for you, Carla. Believe that."

* * *

Jenny enjoyed the video presentation, but only because it gave her valuable insight into the ones she would produce once she got the contract for Valhalla's PR program. Deliciously, she thought how, no doubt, free cruising on board their ships would also be part of the deal. Kirk said that sometimes he was assigned to other vessels; perhaps they could arrange her business trips with his tours of duty. So many options, she thought happily, confident that the future had never looked so bright.

At twelve-thirty, she went to Kirk's cabin. She knocked on the door, but there was no answer, so she used her key. Just inside, on the coffee table, she saw the note he had left. She read that he was working an extra shift for the officer who would fill in for him on the day scheduled for the Briskdal glacier hike. He would see her at seven-thirty.

Jenny let herself out again and locked the door behind her.

Deciding to have lunch in the dining room, she found only Steve at the table, and he was thrilled she had showed up.

"It worked!" he cried, standing to hold out the chair next to him, grinning from ear to ear, his eyes shining.

She had to laugh. "*What* worked? Is this sea air getting to you, Steve?"

"No, *you* are," he boldly declared, "and what worked was *magic*. You see, I was standing at the railing a little while ago, and I saw a bottle floating in the ocean, so I borrowed a rope from one of the crew and fished it out, and what do you know? A beautiful genie popped out and said she would grant me one wish. I could've wished for a million dollars, you know, incidental stuff, but I said no, I'm gonna go for the very best! I want Jenny Denton to show up for lunch so I can have another chance to try and impress her with what a great guy I am."

He was still standing, waving his arms dramatically, and Jenny burst into laughter and told him he looked ridiculous and to sit down before the men in white coats came to take him away.

"I *am* glad you're here, and I don't care who knows it!" He sat down, waved at Miguel, and told him to send the waiter from the bar over with a bottle of champagne.

"Champagne?" Jenny blinked, still laughing. "For *lunch*?"

"What else does one drink when one is with an angel?"

Jenny shook her head. "You're hopeless."

"No!" He wagged a finger. "I am *help*less—helplessly mad about you, and I figure I don't have much time left on this cruise to convince you that *I'm* the man for you—not your fair-haired sailor. His mistress is the sea. I don't happen to have one."

Jenny was relieved not to feel pressured, could enjoy Steve's new, light mood and careless banter.

"So, why didn't you go ashore today?" he wanted to know.

"Because I did the whole Oslo tour yesterday, and I just wanted to relax on board today."

"Well, I'm glad you did. I sure welcome your company."

After lunch, they walked aimlessly around the ship, enjoying the splendor of the sea, delighting in people-watching, window-shopping, an ice-cream cone. They saw an Eddie Murphy film in the theater and laughed till tears ran down their cheeks. When the movie was over, it was nearly three o'clock and teatime on the international deck, which meant open-faced sandwiches and a variety of cookies and pastries. They each filled a plate, unable to resist, and Steve suggested they go to his cabin, where he had a bottle of wine chilling in the little refrigerator.

His cabin was on the same deck as Jenny's but at the

opposite end of the ship. Steve opened the wine, and by the time they finished eating, the bottle was nearly empty. He ordered another from room service, over Jenny's protests that she was doing what she always did when she had too much wine—giggling and being silly. He said, nonsense, he adored her, and, besides, how could he seduce her unless he got her drunk?

She knew he was teasing, and they continued to enjoy each other, talking about so many things they realized they had in common. Since they frequented the same restaurants and clubs in Atlanta, they could not believe they did not remember ever seeing each other. Jenny was not a Falcons fan but finally admitted she had always wanted to go to a game. Steve reminded her of his invitation to the opener. She hedged, and finally said, "We'll see." He vowed he was not going to give up on her, and she laughed and said she was well aware of that fact.

When the second bottle of wine was gone, Steve picked up the phone to order another. Firmly, but a bit dizzily, Jenny got to her feet, headed for the door, and said, "No way! I've had plenty, thank you, and it's time to get dressed for dinner."

"Tonight is formal, you know." He opened the door for her and hopefully asked, "Can I have a dance after dinner before your sailor whisks you away from me?"

Regretting having to dash his hopes, she said, "Sorry, but I'm invited to a party in Oslo being given by the Valhalla executives. Maybe tomorrow night?"

Determined to keep things light, because he'd decided being so serious was driving her away, Steve kept the smile pasted on his face. "Well, okay. Good luck, by the way. I know this is important to you."

"It sure is. Thanks. And I had a wonderful time this afternoon."

"Maybe tomorrow night I can finish seducing you,

make you fall in love with me, get married, have lots of kids . . ."

She laughed and hurried away. Steve, bless his heart, might fancy himself falling in love with her, but *she* was counting the hours till it was time to fall into the arms of her own special love.

But inside a nagging voice reminded her that the clock really *was* ticking and she had to come to terms with all her dreams *and* her fears before the ship reached Amsterdam. She wanted to admit to being totally and helplessly in love with Kirk, but the churning question continued to nag within: Did she dare?

_________________ **SIXTEEN** _________________

Jenny wore a form-fitting gown and dazzled the men at the Valhalla dinner party with her beauty, charmed their wives with her wit and intelligence. Kirk made the perfect escort, and no one could have guessed they were more than business acquaintances. In a private meeting with his uncle and two other executives, she presented her ideas in capsule form, showed them her rough draft for a new brochure and catalog, and went over other ideas. They were unanimously impressed and said that when she had a firm proposal in writing, they saw no reason she could not have the contract if they could agree on the financial terms.

Jenny was on cloud nine and could not help teasing Kirk that it appeared she would've got the contract even if she hadn't slept with him. Enjoying her triumph, he teased, "Yeah, well, you can't be sure. I might have told them behind your back just how great you are." And they laughed together.

The dinner was sumptuous and everything went well. A string trio played for dancing afterward, but Kirk apologetically reminded Jenny he had to get back to the ship in preparation for sailing.

It was only eleven when they got back on board, and he said he should be off duty around one. "I've just got some paperwork to take care of, check over the nautical charts, see what's come over the radio lately. You go enjoy yourself, make all the men's eyes pop out, and I'll meet you back in my cabin and then we'll go dancing. Okay?"

They were on the elevator, alone once more, and she melted against him. They kissed till they were breathless, then he forced himself to push her away. "Oh, Jenny, my love," he whispered, "what am I going to do without you? Three more days, and then you leave me."

Wanting to lighten the moment, for she was so shaken by the desire ripping through her body at his nearness, she teased, "Well, there's always another cruise, and I'm sure you'll have your choice of lonely female passengers to keep you company."

His eyes burned intensely into hers. "Don't even joke about that, Jenny," he said tightly. "You're the only woman I want."

"But isn't there someone out there who thinks you belong to her?" she could not resist asking again. "After all, we both know how you keep secrets," she bantered.

Solemnly, he shook his head. "No. There's only you, Jenny, and that's the way I want it." And Kirk felt that he was being completely truthful. The others did not matter. Never really had. His heart had been free—till now.

He got off the elevator on his deck, and hurried to change into his work uniform. Jenny pushed the button, wanting to get the overnight bag from her cabin that she'd packed earlier with slacks and a sweater. She didn't want to have to walk through the ship in the morning hours wearing her gown.

The doors swished open, and she realized she was on the main deck. Passengers were milling about, since the theater was just letting out. It had been a formal night on board, and everyone was wearing their finest. A few people got on the elevator with her, and just as the doors were about to close again, she heard her name being called excitedly.

"Jenny, Jenny! There you are, and, my God, you're gorgeous." Steve stepped out of the crowd to pull her gently from the elevator. His gaze sweeping to devour her, he murmured, "You're stunning. Absolutely stunning. And I refuse to let you go anywhere 'til you have a drink with me and tell me how everything went tonight with the VIP's."

She thought, why not? The hour was not late. She had some time to kill 'til Kirk got off duty.

They went into her favorite of the lounges—the Starlight. Furnished in gold and white and pink, it was a quiet, romantic place. They took a table by a window, overlooking the sparkling sea in the mystic light. Steve ordered white wine, and she excitedly recounted the evening. He listened, impressed, sharing her enthusiasm, then said, "I'm really, really happy for you, Jenny. And this is just the beginning, I know. You'll have an international account, and that carries a lot of prestige. You're really on your way!"

They toasted her success, and, of course, he reminded her of his willingness to help in any way possible. "And remember," he added in a serious tone, "when we get back to Atlanta, we're going to be friends, right?"

"Right!" she assured him. More than that, she could not promise, felt she'd made that understood.

They had more wine, talked on, and time slipped away. Suddenly, with a glance at her watch, Jenny said she had to go. Steve frowned, because he had a pretty good idea of just where was she was going, but he dared not make a comment. Though it still infuriated him she was seeing the "white wolf," he'd decided the best thing to do was keep his mouth shut. After all, when the cruise was over, they would be back in Atlanta together, and the white wolf would still be on the ship. Then it would be *his* turn, and he intended to make the most of every moment.

He walked her to the elevator, then said he thought he'd stop by the casino and see how Carla and Russ were getting on. "She seemed upset at dinner," he confided. "I'm afraid that guy is really taking her for a ride."

"Well, that's something she's got to realize for herself," Jenny said. "She's sweet and I like her and she deserves better."

Hurrying to get her overnight bag, she then made her way to Kirk's cabin. The instant she let herself in with the key he'd given her, she spotted the note propped against a bucket filled with ice and a bottle of wine chilling.

She picked up the note and read; "Sorry, but I've a little more work to do. Enjoy the wine, and I'll be back as soon as I can." Then he had closed, "Jeg elske deg. Kirk."

Smiling, feeling all warm inside, she wondered what the Norwegian words *Jeg elske deg* meant. She would be sure to ask Kirk, had a feeling it was something wonderful.

The wine was open, so he must have left it only a short while ago, having come to the cabin to leave the note. She poured a glass, sipped it as she walked about the sitting area looking at the pictures on the wall. Nautical prints. Maps of the Caribbean. Her foot bumped into her bag so she decided to take it back to the sleeping alcove. The light was on. She set it down by the bed, turned to go, then saw that the closet door was ajar. The cover of a *People* magazine leaped out at her. It was an old issue she had not read, and she was hungry to read something in English. Kirk's magazines were all in Norwegian.

She knelt to pick it up, then froze.

Beneath, on the floor, in a loose pile, were too many letters to count in a glance. Thirty. Forty. She could see different handwriting, different postmarks, and the return addresses were headed by women's names.

She stood, only vaguely aware of the way her legs were shaking. The magazine dropped from trembling fingers. *He had said there was nobody special,* she comforted her suddenly suspicious mind. That meant none of those letters from any of those women meant anything. *But dear Lord, so many!*

At once, above the roar that had begun inside, she knew she should put the magazine back lest he come in and see it moved, and know she had seen his mail. It was best to let it go, forget it. It was none of her concern.

She knelt once more, to put the magazine carefully back exactly where she had found it, but then one particular envelope caught her eye. It had been opened, as they all had, but there was the corner of a photograph sticking out of this one. With hands that seemed to have a will of their own, her fingers slowly withdrew the snapshot. Her eyes grew wide, and she gasped as she saw the woman, naked, in a provocative pose. Across the bottom was scrawled: "To my Viking lover. Remember how good you feel inside me! See you soon. Kisses. Marla."

Jenny did not know how long she knelt there but was sadly aware of the true meaning of just what Pandora had done when she opened her box to unleash the miseries of the world. How she wished, tears streaming down her face, that she had never reached for the magazine, for then she would have gone on living in her fool's paradise. But no! It was best to know the truth now—that Kirk had lied. Better to find out this way, than the way she had with Bryan.

Bitterness quickly engulfing to obliterate the pain, Jenny got to her feet, grabbed her overnight bag, and started to run out of the cabin, then suddenly stopped. Rage burning through her veins like molten lava, she reached to her neck and yanked the chain, breaking it, that held the little pewter ship Kirk had given her. She dropped it on the table, then placed his key beside it. To hell with locking the door behind her. Let someone walk in and steal his porn collection!

She slammed out, not caring that she bumped right into Lars Ingebretsen as he was squiring his girlfriend into his cabin. They both looked at her in alarm, for she was a sight—eyes wide with her anger, face flushed with the venom of her rage.

Jenny was all the way back to her suite and standing in front of the door before she remembered she had promised to stay away all night. Standing there with her overnight bag, she realized she had nowhere to go.

She stood there a moment, stewing over what to do, and finally decided that for the time being she would just go back to the disco and have a drink. There was a utility closet just down the hall and the cabin steward was gone for the night, so she set her bag inside. No need to look any more ridiculous than she felt by walking around carrying it.

The instant she entered the noisy, crowded disco, Steve spotted her and rushed over to cry joyously, "I can't believe it! You're here. Alone. Without the sailor. You came back because you realize you love me, right? Let's find the captain and get married now! Tonight."

She forced a small laugh, for Steve was a delight since he'd replaced pressuring her with humor, but, inside, she was crying. She let him lead her to his booth, where he'd been sitting alone. After the waiter brought the stiff drink Steve had sensed she needed, he discarded his mask of vivacity and soberly, bluntly, asked, "Would you like to talk about it?"

"I don't know," she whispered as she took a swallow of the drink. "I don't think I can."

He put his arm around her and gently assured her, "Well, I'm here when you think you can."

She gave him a wan smile of appreciation, then concentrated on consuming the drink as quickly as possible in hopes of drowning the pain . . . the image of that vulgar picture with its brazen inscription.

She was having her second drink, with Steve devotedly waiting for her to open up to him, when he suddenly stiffened and said, "Well, well, look who's here."

Jenny looked up to see Kirk towering above them, his face grim as he ignored Steve and tersely directed himself to her. "Let's go where we can talk, Jenny."

She swallowed past the lump of rage in her throat. "I have nothing to say to you."

"Well, I've got a few things I want to clear up with *you*." He moved to sit down next to her in the booth.

At once, Steve moved to protest fiercely, "Hey, buddy! You heard the lady. She doesn't want to talk to you."

Kirk regarded him coolly. "Stay out of this, sir," he then gently advised.

"Oh, yeah?" Steve got to his feet. "I'm a paying passenger, buddy. So is she. I'll just bet this ship has rules about officers making nuisances of themselves.';'

"I don't want any trouble," Kirk tersely declared. "I'm just trying to straighten something out with Miss Denton."

"Yeah, well, we'll see about that!"

He hurried away to find someone with whom to lodge his complaint before Jenny could move to stop him. She didn't want trouble, only wanted to be left alone. She started to get up, but Kirk caught her arm and held her back. "Listen to me, please, Jenny," he begged. "Ingebretsen called me on the bridge, told me he'd seen you storming out of my cabin, that you seemed upset, thought it might have been because you saw him taking that girl into his cabin. I can't control what he does, or any other officer—"

"Well, you all seem to be alike anyway," she snapped.

"Because he runs around on his wife?" he countered incredulously. "Jenny, you're an intelligent woman, and you know that there are men who'll be unfaithful to their wives *regardless* of their profession. You can't judge me because of him. I'm not married!"

"But you lied to me," she said through clenched teeth. "You're nothing but a womanizer, Kirk Moen. I saw your porn pictures!"

"Jenny, please. Let me explain—"

"Explain what?" she lashed out furiously. "First, you don't tell me who you really are, as if you're worried I'm a gold-digger! Then you tell me there's nobody special, and I stumble across your cache of . . . of *fan* letters!" she hotly stammered. "And your vulgar pictures! No, there's nothing to explain. I was just another cruise groupie to you! But no more! I never want to see you again, Kirk Moen. Just leave me alone!"

With that, she jerked free of him, leaped to her feet, and ran out of the disco, leaving him staring after her.

Reaching the lobby outside, she saw that Steve was on the house phone, furiously demanding someone to connect him with the captain, that he had a complaint about one of his officers making a scene in the disco.

Jenny slammed down the button on the phone and cried, "There's no need for this, Steve. Let it go. Besides, I need your help for something else."

He blinked, confused but eager to do anything for her.

Quickly she told him of the agreement she had with Carla. "I have nowhere to go," she explained. "May I sleep on the floor in your cabin? Just for tonight?"

He took her hand in his, nodding with compassion. "Jenny, I'm your friend. You take the bed. I'll take the floor."

She hurried him away from the disco, wanting to be gone before Kirk came out.

SEVENTEEN

When Jenny awoke, she did not at first know where she was. She sat up to glance about wildly, then saw Steve curled up asleep in a chair, a blanket wrapped around him, and it all came painfully flooding back.

They had left the disco and come to the cabin. Steve had asked no more questions, just ordered coffee, which she declined. He had loaned her pajamas so she would not have to sleep in her nice clothes and she had changed in the bathroom. He tucked her in his bed, then impulsively kissed her, but she had not responded. It was as though she were dead inside, could feel no emotion for anyone or anything. He was disappointed but did not push himself, just moved to the chair where he had finally fallen asleep.

I just won't let any of it matter, Jenny told her grieving heart. *I won't look back. I'll try to see it as just being fun while it lasted, but that's all it was—fun!*

Kirk, she bitterly mused, probably collected women like some people collect stamps or miniatures. He was an officer on a love boat, and he played the game and played it well. Beautiful though it was, she had taken it all too seriously and was angry with herself for allowing her emotions to run away with her. It was another bitter lesson learned, but then, she'd not been wise to the ways of Fantasy Land! And so what? Why should she condemn those who *did* play the game? After all, *they* knew the rules, the consequences. But now that *she* did, although by a painful lesson, she wanted no further part of any of it.

Yet, despite her reasoning and rationalizing, Jenny knew there was one undeniable truth—she *did* love Kirk Moen . . . and it would take a long time, if ever, to forget him.

"Hey, good morning!" Steve sleepily greeted, stretching from his cramped position.

Jenny apologized at once. "I shouldn't have slept there, Steve. It wasn't fair for you to give up your bed for me."

"Oh, that's no problem." He pretended to be deeply agitated. "But I have to admit it blows my male ego to smithereens that I wasn't in it *with* you. If this ever gets out, it'll ruin my reputation!"

Despite her misery, Jenny had to smile. Steve was a good friend, and she knew she was forever in his debt. Where could she have gone otherwise? Certainly she couldn't have wandered about the ship all night or made her bed on a sofa in one of the lounges. The last resort would have been to knock on her own door and apologize to Carla for her change in plans, and that would have been an awful thing to do.

"I'm going to order breakfast," Steve was saying, reaching for the phone, "then we're going to have a great day. I was looking at the schedule for today after you fell asleep last night, and there's all kinds of fun things planned—a 'white elephant' auction for people to try and get rid of all the souvenirs they bought on impulse and don't want to drag home, bingo for some nice prizes, a wine-tasting party, movies. We'll have a ball, believe me.''

Jenny felt like getting up and giving him a hug because he was being so wonderful. When he had finished ordering coffee, juice, pastry, waffles, and bacon, she tried to tell him just how grateful she was.

He assured her it was not necessary, asking what friends were for anyway.

They talked, went over the schedule, and picked out the activities they wanted to participate in. All the while, Jenny was determined not to think about what had happened. It was over. *Finis!* There would be time later to grieve for what might have been. For the rest of the cruise, she was determined to have a good-time—even though she was crying on the inside, her heart broken into bits and pieces.

After they had eaten, Jenny said she would go back to her place, change, then meet him for the auction.

When she got to her door, the Do Not Disturb sign was still in place. Well, too bad, she thought. She had kept her end of the bargain and stayed away till the agreed-upon hour. She was about to turn the key when the cabin steward appeared with her overnight bag. He said he had found it in his closet, saw her name on the tag. She thanked him, waited till he went away to push the door open, silently hoping Russ was gone and Carla had merely forgotten to turn the sign around.

Jenny looked inside, hesitated, then rushed in to cry, ''What on earth—''

Carla looked up at her with red and swollen eyes from where she sat at the table by the window. She was still wearing her formal clothes from the night before. A bottle of unopened wine sat in a bucket of stagnant water from melted ice cubes. The tray from room service was untouched—the cheese dried and cracked on soggy crackers. Candle wax was a burned-out glob in the holders, which spilled over onto the table.

Carla was barely able to speak. Her throat was raw, swollen, from the long hours of anguished crying as the night of torment had slowly passed. "He . . . he moved in with Roberta. She . . . she made a scene in the casino when I tried to get him to leave with me. She . . . she said I couldn't afford a man with Russ's tastes, but *she* could. I told her . . ." she continued after pausing to choke on a dry sob that escaped from the depths of her wretched soul, "that . . . that she was trying to *buy* him, like he was a *gigolo*, and you know what she did, Jenny?"

Jenny felt her own tears begin to sting as she stared down at her in pity, whispered hoarsely, "No, Carla. Tell me. Get it out. Share the pain, please."

"She said . . ." she hiccupped, swallowed hard, shook her head as though unable to believe the intensity of her own misery, "She laughed in my face, said I was a fine one to talk, that *I* had tried to buy him, only I couldn't afford him, that Russ had told her how my credit card company wouldn't authorize another cash advance. He *told* her that, Jenny. And they laughed about it."

Kneeling beside her, taking Carla's hands in hers, Jenny implored, "Please. Don't let them do this to you, Carla. Tell yourself it doesn't matter. He's not worth it . . ."

Carla shook her head again, trying to grasp everything that had happened, to understand somehow how it *could* have—where and what, she had done wrong. "He . . . he said I wasn't sophisticated enough for him, that he needed a real woman, like Roberta, who knew how to treat a real man, and—"

"Stop it!" Jenny all but screamed at her then. "Don't do this to yourself, Carla. Don't let him make you do it. He's not worth it. He was using you all along, but you were too kind and innocent and trusting to realize it. Be glad you found out now rather than later, after he took you for everything you had.''

Carla stared at her incredulously, then admitted, ''But he already *did*, Jenny. He lost big in the casino, and I covered his losses and staked him to try to win it back. I ran up charges on my credit card I won't be able to pay, even if I use everything I got out of my divorce. He said he'd pay me back, only now he says he doesn't have the money and never did, and he thought it was understood he was making bets for me, because I don't know anything about gambling and if he'd won, I'd have got the money back and then some, but him losing was just the chance I took.''

The conniving bastard, Jenny silently swore. Oh, how she would like to get her hands on him that very minute. But the present need was Carla and her pain. ''Listen. It will all work out. Somehow. You've got to tell yourself that.''

Jenny was able to get her undressed and into bed, then she phoned room service for hot tea and soup. She called Steve to explain something had come up and she would have to miss the auction but would try to meet him for lunch. He asked if it had anything to do with Carla, and she was able to confirm that it did without letting Carla know they were discussing her. He then confided he guessed as much, because he'd gone to the gift shop for something and saw Russ coming out with Roberta. They were openly affectionate, he said, hugging and kissing, and Russ was showing off a new diamond-and-gold insignia ring, obviously just purchased from the jewelry counter by Roberta.

Jenny bit her tongue, not about to say anything in front of Carla. She hung up, went to sit by the bed and listen if Carla wanted to talk. She didn't, and, finally, after drinking the tea, fell asleep.

Jenny didn't want to leave her, yet did not want to stay in the cabin. She feared Kirk would call and try to cajole her into some fairy tale he would have made up by then to try to explain that awful picture with its inscription. But as time passed and the phone didn't ring, she couldn't help but be puzzled by his silence. She bitterly reminded herself not to care.

It was nearly two o'clock when a knock on the door awoke Carla as Jenny hastened to answer. It was Steve, looking anxious, wanting to know if he could come in. "I got worried when you two didn't show up for lunch."

"I don't intend to go back to the dining room for the rest of the cruise," Carla said somberly. She propped herself against the pillows, jutting her chin up and blinking back fresh tears. "I don't intend to leave this cabin till we get to Amsterdam."

Steve hastened to inform her that would not be necessary if she wanted to avoid Russ. "Miguel told me at lunch he'd moved over to Roberta's table for the rest of the cruise."

Carla squeezed her eyes shut, clenched her fists, and whispered, "I just wish I knew what I'd done wrong—"

"You didn't do anything wrong," Steve cried. "Hey, listen, Carla, I had that guy pegged from the start. He's a creep, and he uses people. If that old bag doesn't realize he's latched onto her for her money, then she's a fool."

"Oh, she knows, all right," Jenny was quick to tell him. "According to Carla, she's *proud* of the fact!"

Steve just shook his head, then went to sit next to Carla on the bed and urge, "I don't think you should let this ruin the rest of your trip. Chalk it up to experience and try to forget it. There're lots of things to do today, and tomorrow is a full schedule, too.'' He turned to Jenny. ''I hear they're scheduling another auction since the one this morning was such a success!''

''But tomorrow is the trip to the glacier,'' she reminded him.

He frowned. ''Listen, I've been thinking about that, and from what I hear, it's a pretty strenuous trip. It's kind of steep going in places, and when you get to the top, you can't really get near the ice. Too dangerous. I think we'd all be better off staying here and looking at it from a distance, then we can have fun on board while everyone else wears themselves out.''

Jenny thought of how Kirk had described what it was like to reach the Briksdal glacier, the hallowed experience of looking down into the dazzling blue-and-purple depths of ice that had been there thousands of years was sacred . . . like bearing witness to the very creation of the universe. She knew she wanted that encounter, for it was the end of the journey and would signify her final farewell to a dream and manifest her return to reality. ''I'm going,'' she said adamantly. ''You two can do what you want.''

Carla didn't speak, just stared out the window at the rolling gray ocean, as though making decisions of her own, not to be confided or shared with anyone else.

''If *you* go, *I* go,'' Steve sighed, then said, ''Hey, I almost forgot. There's something really special about to happen on deck. They've got a Norwegian helicopter flying up to the glacier to bring back a big chunk of ice in a net. They're going to land it in the kiddie pool, on the aft deck, then chip it off so everybody can have a taste.''

Jenny thought that sounded like a rare treat and leaned over to give Carla's shoulder a shake. ''Come on,'' she urged. ''What do you say?''

Carla shook her head. ''No. I'm tired. I want to stay here. You two go ahead. I'll be fine.''

Jenny did not want to leave but thought Carla might nap if they got out and left her alone. It seemed she had been up all night, anyway. "Okay. We'll bring you a piece."

"No need."

Jenny exchanged a concerned look with Steve and got up to go with him. They were almost to the door when Carla faintly called to her.

"I plan to stay in bed the rest of the day . . . don't want to go out tonight, but . . ." she drew in her breath raggedly, then let it out slowly, "I *would* like to go with you to the glacier tomorrow, if that's okay."

"Of course it's okay!" Jenny cried, relieved to see a little spirit. She hurried back to give her a hug. "We'll have a great time," she assured her. "You'll see."

Carla mutely nodded, tried to smile, but instead turned her face to the pillow.

Out in the hall, Jenny confided to Steve, "I'm worried about her. That creep really did a number on her."

"She'll be fine," he said, then cautiously asked, "How about you?"

Not about to discuss her own misery, she gave a firm nod. "I'll be fine, too," she shrugged. "No problem."

"Look," he gestured helplessly, "I don't want to pry, but it doesn't take an idiot to figure out you and that guy had a falling out. Frankly, I'm glad, but if there's anything I can do—"

"Nothing," she told him. "I just want to forget it."

He smiled with relief and happiness. It was his turn now, and he intended to make the most of it.

They went outside and up two flights of stairs to stand at the crowded railing. A helicopter was hovering over the ship, and they watched with interest as it slowly, carefully, lowered the net-encased chunk of glacial ice.

Excitedly, Steve said, "I'm going to go down there and get in line to get us a sample." He hurried away.

A woman standing next to Jenny remarked, "You know, they say those things are thousands of years old."

Jenny turned to respond politely at the precise moment she heard a familiar accent say, "Perhaps even millions, since the creation, some say."

Jenny froze. Kirk was standing on the other side of the woman.

Looking directly at Jenny, he continued to address himself to the other woman. "Glaciers are large bodies of perennial ice, fed by snow from an area of accumulation above the snow line, and the snow being compressed into ice." He went on with interesting details.

Jenny could not help the familiar tremor within, fired by his nearness—just as she could not help thinking what a fool she'd been. She tore from his penetrating gaze, refusing to see the hurt and question in the blue depths.

The woman focused her camera on the distant glacier, clicked the button, then smiled gratefully up at Kirk, "Thank you, Officer. You've been very interesting to talk to."

She walked away, and Jenny started to, as well, but Kirk moved quickly to her side and clamped his hand down on her arm and almost fiercely whispered, "You aren't going anywhere till you tell me what this is all about, Jenny."

She glared at him, shaking from head to toe with indignant fury as she let him have it. "It's about white wolves, Officer Moen, who turn cruises into consecutive one-night stands for stupid women like me!"

Again, she tried to move away, but he held fast. "I can see you've been talking to Paula Streeter in the gift shop."

Jenny's eyebrows shot up in mock surprise. "Oh? Is *she* a member of your fan club, too?"

"Hardly. She hates all the officers, since she threw herself at one her first week at her job and he was married, wouldn't leave his wife for her. So she takes out her hatred on all of us. I think she's gone too far, and it might be time to recommend she be terminated."

"That won't stop the talk," Jenny snapped, "There are probably lots of girls like me who live to tell the tale!"

"*What* tale?" he cried, incredulous. "Jenny, I never deceived you. I meant everything I said. I still do."

"You said there was no one special."

"There isn't."

"Then what about the letters and that picture?"

"I never told you there weren't other women in my life before you, and I have no control over what they write to me, *or* the photographs they send, and, frankly . . ." he paused to take a deep breath before daring to remind her, "it really wasn't any of your business, Jenny."

"You're right! It wasn't . . . and it isn't. So leave me alone!"

"But I have to make you see all that's history. I haven't asked you how many men *you* might have slept with in the past."

From the corner of her eye, she saw Steve just as he looked up from his place in line waiting for a sample of the glacial ice. At once, spotting Kirk, he headed fast in their direction. "Just leave me alone," she furiously repeated.

"Sure. If that's the way you want it." He released her then to look down at her solemnly with eyes narrowed. "But I'll tell you something, Jenny. I think you were looking for an excuse to break up with me. I thought you were different. I thought you were a mature woman, not like the others who come on board to have a fling they can leave behind and not feel guilty over when they return to their real worlds."

She shook her head in protest. "I wasn't looking for a fling."

"I wonder. I remember how you blew me away that first night we made love, when you said maybe it was Bryan you were making love to and not me. Maybe you were right. That *might* explain your behavior."

She was dangerously close to tears. Her heart was hurting at his nearness and she had a strong desire to throw herself in his arms and pretend none of it had ever happened. "I cared about you, damn it. I wanted it to work out for us, but I should've known it couldn't. We live in two different worlds."

"I don't think that's it, at all. I think the truth is that you aren't ready for love. With me or any other man. But when it comes to your career, you'll take any risk to succeed. In matters of the heart, you're scared to chance anything."

"That's not true," she argued. "It's not—"

"Maybe one day," he sharply interrupted, "you'll find out life isn't merely a caricature, and that dreams don't come true unless you're willing to take a few chances and work at making them come true. The same as with your career.

"*You*, Jenny Denton," he rushed on, a nerve in his jaw twitching, blue eyes sparkling with his own indignity, "are a *coward* when it comes to romance, and while I'll never forget you, I'm afraid I'll always remember you with pity, and also think we *were* just like ships that pass in the night!"

With that cold, perfunctory declaration, Kirk turned on his heel and briskly walked away.

Jenny stared after him, shaken. Her first impulse was to rant and rave and scream that he was wrong-wrong-wrong. She *could* love, *did* love, only she was too proud to let any man make a fool of her as he had done. For heaven's sake, the only reason he had time for her on this cruise was because none of his harem was on board and he happened to meet *her* before he spotted other prey.

But she said none of those things, for the anger was dissipating into mingled feelings of confusion and sadness.

Suddenly Steve stormed up to demand, "Hey, was that guy bothering you again? I swear this time I *am* going to the captain. He's got no right—"

"No." Jenny was firm. "It's over. There's no need. He won't be bothering me again."

Except in my broken dreams, her heart silently cried, *and when I think of what might've been . . .*

_________________ **EIGHTEEN** _________________

Jenny had spent a restless night, unable to push Kirk's accusations from her mind.

He was wrong.

She had *not* been looking for an excuse to end their relationship.

And she was *not* afraid to love.

He was only trying to hurt her to defend himself. She *would* not, *could* not, accept his diatribe.

Several times during the long night, she had heard Carla crying into her pillow but decided it best to just leave her alone, let her work it out herself. She had stayed in the cabin, would not eat the dinner Jenny had sent in to her. Yet she insisted she was going to the glacier.

At last, the morning dawned bright and clear. Jenny tried to cheer Carla, telling her what a great day they were going to have—but to no avail. Carla was very quiet, morose, all vestiges of her once sunny personality gone.

"It's a long tour," Jenny reminded her. "I think you should have something to eat, so I told Steve we'd meet him for breakfast."

"I'm not going back in the dining room," Carla reminded her dully. "I don't want to run into Russ or Roberta."

"We're not going into the dining room. We're meeting him on deck to eat out there. Get your jacket and come on. We have to be ready to board the tenders to go ashore in half an hour." She felt as though she were dealing with a child, because, other than her refusal to go to the dining room, Carla was completely docile and passive.

With Steve also encouraging, Carla drank a cup of coffee, nibbled on a doughnut; then it was time to leave.

"It's a *nine*-hour tour," Steve groaned. "I still think we should cash in our tickets and spend the day doing something relaxing."

Carla surprised them by showing enough spirit to firmly protest, "No! I'm going. It's something I want to do . . . something I *have* to do."

"And I feel the same," Jenny firmly chimed in. "If you don't want to go with us, Steve, don't."

He sighed, shrugged, said he'd go along, but not to blame him later when they were exhausted, had blisters on their feet, and felt like hell for the time remaining on the cruise.

After riding a bus for over an hour, they reached the shores of the Hornindalsvatnet, Norway's deepest lake— with a depth of nearly two thousand feet, the tour guide informed. After a rest stop for coffee, sandwiches, and cookies, they journeyed on to the Briksdal Inn.

Carla had sat next to the window, staring out, and had not spoken a word since boarding the bus. Jenny, next to her, looked across the aisle at Steve and shook her head worriedly.

He ignored her anxiety over Carla, and instead continued his argument. "This is our last chance. We can stay at the inn, nice and cozy, have lunch, a bottle of wine, sit in front of the fire, if they've got one, and let everyone else wear themselves out to go look at a giant freezer that somebody forgot to defrost a million years ago.''

Jenny shook her head. "No. I'm making the hike to the top. Once we get there, the view is worth it.''

"*What* view?'' he cried. "A big chunk of ice that we can see from down here! What's so great about standing next to it?''

Jenny asked where his spirit of adventure was, and he quipped that he'd already worn it out on the bus ride. When they gathered outside, the tour guide, a Norwegian who spoke good English, informed them that while the first hour or so of the hike was arduous, the rest of the way would be fairly easy. There were no sudden, sharp turns; the path was steadily climbing, but smooth. He hoped everyone was wearing good walking shoes, and said that if anyone got tired, they should just stop, rest, or turn back. Lunch would be served at the inn, and it was their option to eat before or after the hike.

"Let's eat now,'' Steve at once suggested.

"And walk that distance on a full stomach?'' Jenny cried. "No way. Let's go.'' Carla, she noted, had already started out, taking quick, purposeful strides. She hurried to catch up and warn her to slow down lest she tire herself out quickly.

Steve started gasping almost from the moment they set out. "I'm just not used to this kind of exertion,'' he groaned defensively. "And it's ridiculous.''

Jenny felt annoyance creeping up on her. The view all around them was breathtaking—above, snowcapped mountains; beyond, sprawling green valleys; below, the sparkling blue waters of the fjord. She wanted to enjoy this, to spend the moments when they stopped to rest in meditation, not listening to Steve's constant griping. She was having enough difficulty as it was fighting the demons within that needled with painful memories—such as how she and Kirk had so looked forward to spending this day *together*. She recalled how the glacial ice served up on deck the day before had crackled and popped when liquid was poured over it like the famed breakfast cereal. Kirk had told her about that, how he intended to bring a small canteen of water from the ship so they could chip away a bit themselves, to witness the sensation at the source. Nature's champagne, he'd called it, to toast to their future. Yet here she was now, miserably trudging along behind a zombielike Carla and a whining Steve.

Finally, she could not resist snapping at Steve, "Maybe this will serve to make you sit up and take notice of the fact you aren't in good shape."

"Good shape?" he echoed, irate at the jab. "Listen, I play golf twice a week, and—"

"And you ride a golf cart, right? You don't walk eighteen holes carrying a bag of clubs. I'm talking *serious* workout, Steve. I thought you said you went to a gym on a regular basis. Sure doesn't look like it now."

"Listen, *Rocky* himself would huff and puff on a climb like this. I've had it!" He suddenly dropped to a sitting position at the side of the trail, folded his arms across his chest like a brooding Indian chief. "I'll be waiting right here when you two Amazons get back."

"Fine!" Jenny said, relieved not to have to listen to his griping anymore. She quickened her pace to catch up with Carla, also wanting to distance herself from him, lest he change his mind.

When at last they reached the top, Jenny was struck by the awesome spectacle. The glare of the shimmering ice in the sunlight was blinding. Due to Carla's fast, determined pace they had arrived way ahead of the other hikers, and they were alone. "We'd better wait till the guide gets here to go any farther,'' Jenny called to Carla. ''I don't think we should go out on the ice by ourselves.''

The glacier stretched like a great white arm to infinity, the dazzling light making it impossible to see beginning or end. Carla was still walking, but had slowed enough to pick her way across the crusty surface. The crevice, with its mirrored walls of blue that Kirk had described, was directly ahead, framed by an ice tunnel. ''Hey, let's wait here,'' Jenny called again, feeling a prickle of fear begin to needle her spine. ''I don't think it's safe. We don't know the regular path, where the ice is hard enough to walk on.''

''I came on this cruise to have a good time!'' Carla suddenly yelled, almost hysterically. ''I've wasted enough time in the casino, the bars, in *bed*. I want to see something. I want a memory to take home besides how I made a damn fool of myself!''

''Well, at least wait for the guide,'' Jenny pleaded again. Carla was about thirty feet ahead of her, picking her way along on the sharp eruptions of ice.

From behind and below, Jenny heard the sound of someone's frenetic calling. Turning, she saw it was the guide, who had broken away from the pack of hikers he had been leading—older people he felt the need to walk with—to hurry towards them. He had seen Carla making her way across the ice to the crevice and was waving and yelling for her to stop, turn back—repeating Jenny's warning it was not safe to go alone, that she did not know the trail.

''Did you hear him?'' Jenny cupped her hands to her mouth and shouted, truly alarmed; ''Turn back, Carla. You could fall.''

''Would that be so bad?'' she yelled then, twisting her head to look at her and challenge. ''What have I got to go back to, anyway? Everything, all my money, gone. Maybe I'd be better off if I did just fall in that big hole. Maybe it *is* the beginning of creation, maybe I'll come back in my next life smarter and men won't make such a fool of me!''

Dear God! The scream could not get past the sudden knot of terror in her throat. Was Carla about to kill herself? It hit her at once—the way she had been so determined to see the glacier firsthand, how steadfastly she had walked—and now she was ignoring the warnings and heading straight into possible disaster.

She couldn't let her do it. Her life wasn't over, not because of some conniving bastard who wasn't worth the energy it took to loathe him. ''Carla, no!'' she cried, gingerly stepping onto the ice and getting her footing. ''Stop. Come back. Wait for me. I'll help you—''

Suddenly, without warning, there was a sound like a tree falling—a great cracking noise that was deafening to behold and growing in intensity. Above the roar came Carla's terrified scream—just before she disappeared from sight in a swooshing crush of splitting, falling ice.

Without thinking, Jenny raced forward, could see that Carla had caught hold of the sudden-formed ledge as she had fallen . . . but already her grasping fingers were losing grip on the ice. ''Carla, hang on, hang on,'' she screamed. ''I'm coming.''

She knelt, and reached out for her. From somewhere came the sound of others yelling, shouting, crying out, and Jenny reached, reached, reached, gasping as, at last, she had hold of Carla's hand, felt the flesh, held on with all her might.

And then the ice beneath her cracked, broke, and Jenny felt herself sliding forward headfirst, had a fleeting glimpse back in time of a schoolyard slide, daring to answer the challenge of her classmates to go down headfirst, and *she was*—into a blue-and-crystal abyss, with the sounds of her screams, and Carla's, bouncing off the frozen walls as they tumbled downward in a hail of cascading ice . . .

Jenny was floating. On a sea of whipped cream. So soft. Like marshmallows. She would raise her arm, only to have it weighted down by the thick cushion of comfort that shielded her from all pain. Did she want to rise up? Was it not better to remain so soft and warm . . . for something was out there waiting. Something terrible. It was cold and sharp, and her throat burned when she had to take a breath into it. Far better to remain where she was. No. Turn. Turn over. So stiff and cold, and—

"Jenny, don't move!"

She felt hands on her, holding her where she was.

"Don't look down."

But she opened her eyes and did so anyway, at once gasping in horror at the yawning blue hole that was waiting to devour.

"We're on a ledge. It's very narrow. We mustn't move. I can hear the ice cracking. It could go any second."

Jenny shook her head to clear it, and suddenly it all came back in a rush, and she knew they had fallen but had obviously landed on a narrow ledge. They were clinging to life—and infinity was a hair's-breadth away. "Are you all right?" she asked Carla as she gingerly touched her own forehead, felt the stickiness, knew it was blood.

Carla was lying next to her, on her side, her face contorted with pain she fought against. "I think my ankle is broken. Some cuts. Bruises. What about you?"

Jenny very carefully made both feet wriggle, her legs, arms, hands—slight movements only but mercifully there. "Nothing broken."

"My head hurts bad."

Jenny noted with alarm that Carla's voice was becoming

slurred, uneven, as though she were losing consciousness. There was light, for the glaring sun above fired the glistening lights of their icy world, perhaps thirty feet below. She could see that Carla's eyes were becoming glassy, then simply stared ahead, unseeing.

Terror was a jolt to her heart as she reached to feel for a pulse, then breathed a sigh of relief to find it. Carla was mercifully still alive but had passed out.

A voice boomed from above. "Can you hear me?"

Jenny craned her neck to look up but could not see the face of the man who had spoken, for the glare was too great. "Yes," she was able to faintly call. "I can hear you."

"Is anyone hurt?"

"Carla . . . she's unconscious." Suddenly there was a cracking noise directly beneath her, and Jenny screamed, "The ice is going to break any second. You've got to get us out!"

"Hang on. Help is on the way. Just be very still."

Jenny could only obey—and pray as she had never prayed before in her life.

The minutes ticked by. Every so often she heard the terrifying sound as the ice cracked maybe a fraction of an inch at a time. How long would it hold? How long before she and Carla were both plunged into eternity? She willed herself not to succumb to tears, for her shudders might set off the last collapse of both spirit and body, as well as the ledge on which she and Carla helplessly lay.

She thought of how she did not want to die. There were so many things left to be tasted in life. She had heard the legend, how a drowning person's life passes before his eyes, but she was not thinking in those desperate moments of any past existence, only what the future might have brought. Flair would have been a success, she had no doubt about that. It dawned on her that never had she feared meeting a career challenge head-on, for it was the secret of her success. Maybe Kirk had been right when he said she was afraid to face the personal challenge of succeeding at love. Now it seemed clear—what she had chosen not to see before, how she and Bryan *had* drifted apart, how it had been her pride that was wounded when she found him making love to Linda, not her heart. For *that*, she came to realize, with amazing clarity, there in her possible grave of ice, she had not given out of fear of losing. If she did not gamble, she did not lose.

So what had been Kirk's intent when he accused her of looking for an excuse to end all that was between them? Of course. It came to her then. He wanted to make her realize that she was actually afraid of giving her heart totally, for fear of *losing*! So what if he'd had other loves yesterday. Did that mean she was not worthy of his tomorrows?

Only now, she acknowledged, fighting to keep from shivering with the cold that enshrouded her and the ever-growing horror of her predicament, it might be too late to learn from her newfound discovery of her own self.

The ice cracked again. The sound lasted longer. The ledge on which they lay actually shifted precariously.

Then, suddenly, like a whisper on the wind, the warm, caressing voice touched her all over. "Jenny, can you hear me?"

It was not real, and surely she was unconscious, like Carla, but she answered, though feebly, all the same, to the chimera of her faltering hope for survival. "Yes . . . yes, I hear you. Help us, please . . ." Was it really Kirk calling to her, or did she just want it to be him so desperately that she imagined it?

The cool, controlled voice was a balm to her.

"I am going to help you, Jenny, but you've got to work with me. Now tell me—are either of you hurt bad?"

"I don't know." Her head, her heart, was pounding with fear, for the ice shifted once more, and hysteria mounted in her voice as she called up, straining to see but still blinded by the light, "You've got to hurry. The ice is going to break any second—"

"Listen to me!" Stern. Forceful. In command. Not her lover, not even her friend. An officer, giving an order. Expecting, demanding it be carried out. "Get hold of yourself. Now tell me. Is Carla conscious?"

"No . . . I think she's fainted."

"Good. She won't be frightened. Now listen very carefully," he repeated in the same, brusque, authoritative tone. "I'm going to lower a rope to you. There's a small hook on the end. I want you to wrap it carefully, but very tightly, around Carla, under her shoulders. Fasten it good. We'll pull her up, then send the rope back for you."

The splitting sound was like a hot needle into her brain, and Jenny screamed, "No. There's no time. The ice is giving way—"

"Stop it!" he ordered tersely. "Now do as I say, and we can get you both out. If you panic, it's all over."

Jenny tensed, waited for what seemed forever until she felt the cold steel of the hook as it gently touched her arm. With quivering fingers, she manipulated it around Carla, securing it as tight as possible. "It . . . it's done," she gasped. "Get her up. Hurry. Please . . ."

"Jenny, listen to me," he called down to her again, an edge to his voice for the first time as the tension of the situation worsened. "When we lift her from the ledge, it may cause the ledge to break all at once. Be ready for that to happen. If it does, grab hold of Carla, the rope, and hold tight. We'll pull you both up. But *do not panic*. Understood?"

She drew in her breath, let it out slowly. "Understood." She was becoming dizzier by the second, and it all seemed like a fog-enshrouded nightmare, none of it real.

"I'm going to count to three. On the count of two, make ready to grab the rope if you hear the ice give. As we hit the count of three we will start to pull her up. Understood?"

She could only nod her head, and he must have seen it, because the next sound she heard was a crisply enunciated "One!"

Her hands began to tremble. She raised her arms toward the rope.

"Two!"

She felt something run from her forehead, into her eyes, blurring her vision—blood from her wound. She could no longer see the rope and groped blindly with her fingertips, just as he pronounced, "Three!"

Beneath her, with one giant snap, the ice collapsed. She lunged for the rope, felt the jerk as it was almost tugged from her desperate grasp.

"Hang on, Jenny, hang on! We've got you both."

Dizzily, Jenny clung tightly, her body pressed against Carla's, legs dangling into nothingness as the sound of the ice echoed forever below them.

Her arms were aching, and she felt as though they had been yanked from the sockets. Pain was burning through her back and spine, but yet she clung, the rope cutting into her flesh. She stared upward into the blinding sunlight, the glare giving her hope that there was life above but below was death, and, dear God, she did not want to die when she had just discovered the courage to face all the wonders life had to offer.

Suddenly she knew she could not hang on any longer. Her fingers were slipping, and she was so weak, so terrified. The sobs were wracking her body, and the pain in her head was getting worse.

She felt herself letting go, unable to cling to the rope . . . to *life* . . . any longer.

NINETEEN

Kirk gritted his teeth at the intense cold against his stomach. Despite the protection of his shirt and jacket, the chill of the ice permeated. The rope was tight around his chest, beneath his shoulders . . . was almost painful.

Behind him, at a safe distance, the tour guide, along with all the other men, stood braced to hold that end of the rope taut.

At his tumultuous shout of Three, they had given a mighty tug to begin hoisting Carla up as Kirk guided. Then he had heard the ominous crack, knew at once that his worst fears were confirmed, that the sudden shift of weight had caused the ledge to reverberate just enough to set off the final rupture.

Jenny had also heard, desperately followed his command, and lunged to hang on to Carla. He felt the burn as muscles strained to obey, every nerve in his body raw and screaming.

"We've got both of them!" he yelled back to the others. "For God's sake, *pull!*"

He could see they were nearing the top and felt a jab

of panic at the sight of Jenny's bloodied face. Her hands were grasping the rope just above Carla's head, and he stretched, reached, trying with all his might to grab for her wrists before she lost her precarious hold.

"Harder!" he yelled hoarsely. "Pull harder!"

She was less than a foot below his reach. He knew pure terror as he caught the movement of her fingers slipping. He had but one brief instant to make his decision to lunge forward, could only hope those behind him were ready for such a sudden jolt and would hold tight or he was going to plunge helplessly into that eternal abyss with them.

A gasp came from the watching crowd as he made his plunge . . . Kirk would later think how his heart stopped beating in that one sheer second when he saw, felt, Jenny drop—just as his hands closed desperately around her wrists.

"I've got her!" he yelled as loudly as he could, trying to be heard above the roar of the Norwegian helicopter *ambulanse* hovering, preparing to land nearby. "Get us out of here before another break!"

With agonizing slowness, they were drawn to a safer point, and Kirk at once got to his knees to cursorily examine Jenny for broken bones. She stirred, moaned, tried to open her eyes against the glaring sun, then closed them and lay still once more.

He felt hands on his shoulders gently pushing him away as the rescue team descended. From somewhere beyond, he heard the tour guide defend himself. "I warned them to wait, but they wouldn't listen, kept right on going, right out on the ice, wouldn't wait for me to lead them the safe way. I was held up by some slow climbers, and those girls, they just took off like bats out of hell!"

Kirk stood back while a paramedic hastily checked Jenny, then, losing patience, he harshly demanded, "How bad is she? I couldn't feel any broken bones, but that cut on her head is still bleeding—"

"Relax . . ." The young man flashed a reassuring smile. "She may have a slight concussion, might need a few stitches, but she's going to be fine."

Kirk breathed a sigh of relief, turned to where Carla lay. "And what about her?"

"Looks like a broken ankle. A few cuts and bruises. She's starting to come around. I'd say both these girls are very lucky. And you are to be commended, sir. We were watching you from the air."

Kirk brushed aside his praise. "Will you be able to transport them back to the ship hospital or do they need a larger facility?" he asked.

"The ship will be fine. I understand the doctor has the means to X-ray and set broken bones. We were in touch with the captain by radio while flying in, and he says you're due in Amsterdam day after tomorrow. They can return with the ship."

Again, Kirk felt a wave of comfort and watched as they carefully positioned the two women onto stretchers and made ready to air lift them. How glad he was he had decided to make the trek, despite the sad personal situation with Jenny. The other men around, he feared, would not have possessed the knowledge necessary to take over and do what had to be done. He did not feel like a hero—only an officer trained to respond to a crisis.

He was about to ask if he could fly back to the ship on the helicopter when the sound of someone yelling hysterically caused him, and everyone else, to turn around. Running toward them, Kirk recognized the man who had become so irate when he had tried to reason with Jenny in the disco.

Red-faced and out of breath, Steve Gentry stumbled the last few steps to the ridge to cry, "What happened? Dear

God, what happened? I heard it was Jenny, and—'' He stopped short, saw her being loaded on board the helicopter and lunged forward. "How is she?" he shrieked. "Is she going to be all right?"

The attendants nodded absently, intent on what they were doing. Kirk moved to try to calm him. "Miss Denton may have a slight concussion," he said. "Miss Sutton a broken ankle. If you'll step back, they're about to take off to fly them back to the ship, and—"

"*You!*" Steve roared, lips curling back in a furious snarl. Doubling his fists, eyes bulging with his rage, he accused, "It's all your fault. You got her all upset. I could tell she wasn't herself, and—"

"Hey! You!" The paramedic who had praised Kirk turned from where he had been buckling Jenny's stretcher inside the aircraft and said, "He's the one who saved these girls. Are you with either one of them?"

Steve's eyes narrowed as his gaze swept over Kirk contemptuously. No matter his heroics, Steve considered him the enemy who stood in the way of his winning Jenny. "Yes," he said tersely. "I am with Miss Denton."

"Then come along. You can ride with us." The paramedic waved him to hurry.

Steve gave Kirk one last gloating look, then rushed to board the waiting helicopter.

The excitement was over and everyone turned back to the original purpose for making the arduous climb—seeing the Briksdal glacier firsthand, up close.

Kirk watched the helicopter rise, begin to make its way back to the fjord and the waiting ship. He had wanted to experience once again the feeling of staring into embryonic creation. Yet since his own existence now seemed meaningless, what did he care how any of this had begun?

He knew he loved Jenny in a way he could never love another woman, but what could he do? Paula Streeter's malicious gossip about white wolves, followed by seeing Ingebretsen fooling around, finally capped by her stumbling across that damn picture of Marla . . . well, he never had a chance. He'd tried to explain, but she wouldn't listen, and now there was nothing left but the pain. Maybe she'd never really loved him at all. Maybe, despite his desperately wanting her to be otherwise, she *was* just like the others, living in a dream world, if only for a little while. But, more than that, he still believed he was right about her being afraid to give her heart to any man.

So sad, he thought, shoulders hunched as he began to make his way back down from the glacier, like ships that pass in the night . . .

Because, God, he loved her so much!

On board the helicopter, Jenny stirred, then moaned. The stretchers were positioned side by side on the floor of the helicopter. Above her, Steve strained against his seat belt to lean down and clasp her hand.

Dry lips parted, and the name she called so desperately was a barely audible whisper. "Kirk . . . Kirk . . ."

Steve frowned. "It's me, *Steve*," he said firmly. "*I'm* here for you, honey, and I always will be. Rest now. Everything's going to be just fine."

She lay still once more.

Jenny's eyes opened to a gossamer world that was tender with gentle sounds, yet frightening with its pungent smells and unfamiliar surroundings. She blinked and tried to focus her eyes, but the veil would not lift. She tried to speak but there seemed to be something pressing down, an unseen hand to stifle any sound she might make.

"Doctor, I think she's coming around."

"Good. I'm almost finished."

"Was it very deep?"

"No. Scalp wounds always bleed a lot. The stitches weren't absolutely necessary, but she might have been left with a worse scar without them. She'll be fine."

"Do you think she has a concussion?"

"No. Everything looks good. I think she just fainted, which isn't surprising, under the circumstances."

Jenny felt as though she had gone back in time, to the summer evening when she would catch a magical lightning bug and run with delight to show her mother her treasure, only to unclasp her fingers to find nothing there. So it was with the rationalization attempted amid the dizziness and fogginess. There were words. People. Lights. But she could not put any of them together to make sense. Elusive. Like the magic bugs.

"Okay. We're all done. Let's move her into that room over there and let her sleep. Stay with her. I've got to set the other one's ankle now."

Jenny felt herself being lifted, lowered, rolled, lifted once more, then the coolness of bed linen. A blanket was tucked around her chin. Someone, a woman, asked if she should have a gown. A man said no. *Let her rest for the moment.*

Lips pressed warmly against her cheek, and Jenny smiled happily. Somewhere a telephone was ringing. Kirk's wake-up call. Time for him to report to duty. Time for her to return to her own quarters. But the night had been beautiful in his strong, loving arms. Together, again and again, they had soared to the stars in ecstasy, and never had she felt so wonderful, so desired, so . . . *loved . . .*

"Jenny, can you hear me?"

It was not Kirk.

There was no deliciously sensual Nordic accent. But there was something familiar in that voice, which reached through the velvet shroud that enveloped her. But who? *Who* was pressing his lips against her cheek?

This time she was able to open her eyes, saw that it was Steve hovering over her, and he broke into a wide grin as she gazed up at him in confusion and bewilderment.

"Hey, sleepyhead. Welcome back to the land of the living. You know you gave all of us a hell of a scare back there."

"Sir, please move . . ." A woman in a white uniform brushed him aside to clamp cool fingers around Jenny's wrist, checking her pulse. Then she began to wrap a blood pressure cuff around her arm.

"What—" Jenny started to speak, had so many questions, but the nurse shushed her till she could finish her reading, then stood back to nod that it was okay for her to talk, for she was doing fine. Then she left them alone.

"How do you feel?" Steve wanted to know.

Jenny thought about that for a moment. How *should* she feel? What was she *supposed* to feel? What was going on?

And then it hit her, all at once, flooding back to terrorize—the ice, the ledge, the fall, Carla, the rope, lifting, what sounded like Kirk's voice, then nothingness. "Carla!" she cried. "How is she? Did they get her out?"

Steve assured Jenny she was fine. "She's in the next room resting. The doc set her ankle. Said it wasn't a bad break, but she'll be in a cast and on crutches for a while.

"You've got a nasty cut on your head," he went on to inform, "but no concussion, like the doc thought at first. He says you'll be sore for a while, but you're a very lucky young lady."

Just then the doctor walked in to check her over once again, to make sure she was, indeed, doing all right. Then he told her he wanted her to stay in the infirmary overnight so they could keep her under observation to make sure they had not missed anything.

"Does your head hurt?" he wanted to know.

"No. I feel a little sore all over, but that's all."

"Great. I'm going to have some food brought in—soup, tea."

He left after answering her questions about Carla, assuring her that she, too, was on the mend. She asked Steve the time, was stunned to learn it was nearly six in the evening. "How did I get back here?"

"You don't remember the helicopter ride?"

"I don't remember anything beyond someone starting to pull us out of that hole and then the cracking sound as the ledge gave way. After that, everything went black." Then, burning to know whether she'd only imagined it was Kirk's voice she'd heard, asked, "The man who was talking to me, telling me to tie the rope around Carla, who was he?"

Steve drew in his breath, then let it out slowly. He was not about to tell her anything about Kirk's part in any of it. "The paramedics took care of everything. Flew you and Carla back here." Then, wanting to change the subject from the actual rescue, went on to say, "The landing on deck was spectacular. The ship's photographer got pictures. It was quite a scene—you, me, and Carla, flying in on a Norwegian flying *ambulanse*."

Jenny sighed with regret. So, it had been her imagination, her mind playing cruel tricks.

"I'm going to look after you now," Steve went on. "We get to Amsterdam day after tomorrow, and I'm going to stay with you every step of the way back to Atlanta. I've already been on the phone in the radio room, and I'll have a car waiting at the airport to take us straight to my place. The housekeeper who comes in when I've got Stevie is going to be there to help me look after you, and—"

"Wait a minute!" Jenny struggled to sit up, pleased to

note she *was* starting to feel like her old self. "You heard the doctor, Steve. I'm fine. Just a bit sore, shaken up. No bones broken. And I certainly don't need to be put to bed at your place, with your housekeeper waiting on me. Thanks, but no thanks."

"I insist." He drew up a chair, sat down, and reached to take her hands in his, holding tight as he looked up at her. He hoped the intensity of his feelings was projected. "Jenny, listen to me. I care about you. Really care about you. I'm pretty sure I'm falling in love with you, if I'm not already—" He gave a nervous laugh.

Jenny seized the moment to interrupt and protest, "Steve, wait, we don't really know each other, and—"

"No!" he cried then, eyebrows jumping up in the desperate insight that it was now or never. She could not escape him for the moment, had no choice but to hear him out, and he had memorized everything he wanted to say to her. "Jenny, you don't understand. You're the woman I've been looking for. You have all the qualities I want—intelligence, background, good looks, poise, charm, everything I need in a wife, a mother for my son and the other children I want to have. You fulfill my every desire. I know it, feel it, and if you're honest with yourself, you'll see it, too. I'm not going to rush you. We need time to really plan things out. But I want to make my intentions clear. I love you, Jenny, and I want to marry you. I *am* going to marry you."

In that instant, Jenny disagreed with the doctor. She *had* had a concussion and she was still unconscious, because all of this was a crazy dream. It could not be happening. She took a long, pitying look at Steve, shook her head slowly and gingerly, tenderly whispered, "No. No, Steve. That's not the way it is, not the way it's going to be. You don't sit down and make a list of what you want in a wife and then go out looking for one in the same way you shop for a new car. You meet someone and fall in love and realize that's the person you were meant to marry. Fate decrees things like that, Steve. Not people.

"And the truth is," she rushed on, not allowing him to interject anything or protest, knowing she was hurting him but not about to be victimized into a stressful situation, "I don't love you. I *like* you. I want to be your friend—but nothing more."

He shook his head, flashed a self-conscious smile. "You'll feel different. I'm going to *make* you love me, and—"

"No, you aren't!" she said, sharper than she intended. "Please, Steve." She tried to soften her tone. "If you persist in your one-sided romance, it's going to make even a friendship between us impossible."

He drew a ragged breath, finally gave a shrug, and said, "Well. Friendship is a start. I guess I'll have to settle for that."

"*Friendship*," she repeated. "Nothing more. And remember, I have no intentions of going home with you. I'm going to my own place. Understood?"

"Let me take you there. In the car I've got waiting."

"That would be nice . . . and *friendly*," Jenny conceded.

The nurse came in to ask whether she needed anything, then suggested Steve run along so she could rest.

When he'd gone, Jenny asked if she could see Carla, was told she was sleeping. "I suggest you do the same," the nurse smiled, going out and closing the door behind her.

Jenny slept again. Her dreams were of Kirk, his breathtaking kisses and tender caresses, the joy and wonder and laughter and excitement they had shared. She relived every moment, and it was wonderful, and when she awoke, she was bitter. The dream was the only happiness. Reality had become stark, harsh, and cruel.

A new nurse looked in, asked if she would like some dinner. Jenny nodded, then dared to inquire if there had been any other visitors for her other than Mr. Gentry. "Let me check the log book," she said. "We keep a list of anyone who comes by or calls."

When she returned a few moments later, Jenny felt a great wave of disappointment to hear there had been no one else.

The dinner tray came. Jenny was not really hungry and merely picked at her food.

The hours ticked by slowly. The infirmary was very quiet. Jenny was restless. She felt fine, just a bit sore where the stitches were. She glanced at the clock on the wall. It was after midnight. No doubt Kirk had heard about the accident. Why didn't he at least call to see how she was? Didn't he care at all?

Finally, she turned her head into the pillow and wept once more . . . for what might have been.

_____________ **TWENTY** _____________

It was the last day of the voyage. The sky was clear, the wind brisk, perfect weather for the ending of, for some, a perfect cruise.

Passengers were busy packing and gathering their things, going to customs briefings to prepare for disembarkation early the next morning. Instructions were given to passengers to leave their luggage outside their cabin doors before retiring so the crew could begin the long and laborious task of transporting to the hold deck for unloading to the dock soon after arrival.

Jenny had spent a restless night in the infirmary. When the doctor came in for a final examination, she was sitting on the side of the bed. She had found her tattered clothes from the day before, was dressed and anxious to be dismissed.

The doctor gave her a prescription for an antibiotic and told her to see her family physician for removal of the stitches in about a week. "You're going to be fine," he finished with a reassuring smile. "You're a lucky young lady."

"And Carla?" she anxiously wanted to know. "How's she doing this morning?"

"I'm on my way to check her now. According to the nurse who was on duty last night, she had some pain with that ankle and had to be given medication. She's still sleeping that off."

Jenny asked if she could see her yet.

He shook his head. "No. Let's let her sleep."

The nurse asked Jenny if she would like a breakfast tray, but she declined, anxious to leave. During the long, miserable night, she'd done some real soul-searching, knew she had to see Kirk one more time. Maybe there would be an explanation that she could accept for that awful picture. And she had to agree with him that he wasn't responsible for what Ingebretsen or any of the other officers did. It was wrong to lump them all into one pile and label them all "white wolves." She could also easily believe that Paula Streeter was bitter and vengeful.

The one thing Jenny now found hard to accept, however, was Kirk's accusation that she was incapable of giving her heart . . . was afraid to love. *That* she did not want to believe, because, in the wee hours of all that self-revelation, she'd come to terms with herself and knew that she *did* love him, and she had to have that last chance to see whether things could be worked out. Because, ultimately, she knew if she got off that ship without seeing him one more time, she'd never forgive herself.

Back in her cabin she ordered coffee from room service before jumping in the shower. Then, dressed in clean slacks and sweater, she sat down at the table to sip the coffee while trying to get her thoughts together as to exactly what she wanted to say. She'd been pretty rough on him, and he might now be angry. Deciding a direct approach was best, she would just ask him to meet and talk. Taking a chance he might still be in his cabin, she picked up the phone and dialed.

There was no answer. It was after eight. No doubt he was on duty. Where to call? The bridge? The engine room? She had no idea, hated to start dialing around at random, for that would look desperate. Well, she *was*, she acknowledged her pounding heart, but no need to let the entire crew know about it!

He'd be in his cabin after twelve, she figured, so she busied herself packing. When that was done, she got Carla's things together, too, brooding about her all the while. She was going to need a friend to help her over the heartbreak, and, after that crazy stunt on the ice, would probably need to go into therapy.

The telephone rang, and Jenny leaped to answer, only to sigh with disappointment at the sound of Steve's voice. "Hey, how are you feeling?" he asked brightly, then rushed on before she could respond. "I called the infirmary. They said you'd been discharged but they were keeping Carla a while longer. I thought maybe you'd like some help packing."

"No, Steve, but thanks for asking. I'm doing just fine."

"Well, how about some company?"

"No, I—"

"It's the last day," he persisted. "A lot of things are going on this afternoon. You need to get out and enjoy yourself."

"Maybe later."

He did not want to give up, but there was no mistaking the firmness in her tone. "Well, how about meeting me for lunch?"

Her stomach gave a rumble. She was hungry, but finding Kirk was more important. "I'm not sure. I may call for a sandwich. I'm still a bit sore from yesterday," she pointed out, hoping he'd take the hint that she was growing impatient with his persistence.

"Well, okay," he murmured reluctantly. "I'll check in with you later."

She hung up, then dialed Kirk's cabin again. No answer.

At five-minute intervals, between noon and one o'clock, she tried to reach him. Finally, she decided that since it was the last day of the cruise, maybe he had a lot of paperwork to do in anticipation of arrival in Amsterdam. But the bottom line, she told herself, was the fact she'd made it quite clear she wanted nothing else to do with him, never wanted to see him again. Maybe *he* was keeping busy so as not to think about *her*! With that sudden optimistic wave of thought, she sat down and wrote him a note. Simple. To the point. "Can we talk? Jenny."

She left her cabin, hurried through the maze of luggage piled in the halls, sidestepping passengers moving about to make the most of their last day of the cruise. She felt good, confident that when Kirk found the note on his door, he'd at least get in touch with her and give her a chance to apologize for being so hasty, and then, *please Lord,* she prayed silently, he'd be able to convince her it was all a misunderstanding, that he did love her, and they could work on the future together. Coming so close to death had made her see many things, the most important of which was to take one day at a time, seize the moment, and don't shut out one single chance for happiness, and . . .

She froze.

She had been about to step from the hallway into the lobby at the elevator bank before the door to the officers' quarters. Now she could only stand with eyes widening, knees trembling, heart pounding.

Kirk was walking through that Officers Only door, but he was not alone. A petite blonde was with him, and just before the door swung shut, Jenny saw him put his arm around her.

She jammed her fist in her mouth to stifle the sobs, turned, and nearly knocked a man down in her haste to get away.

"Hey, why don't you watch where you're going?" he yelled irritably.

"Sorry . . ." she choked, stumbling along, her heart breaking into bits and pieces.

He had not waited till the next cruise! He'd picked up someone else for a little afternoon delight!

The bastard!

She stopped hurrying then, and the pain melted into rage, hot and furious. Not only had he made a fool of her but he was already working on another conquest!

She was still fuming when she got to the door of her suite to find Steve standing there. "Oh, there you are," he grinned self-consciously. "I was afraid you just weren't answering because you knew it was me."

His eyes went curiously to the piece of paper she still held in her hand. She crumbled it into a tight ball and stuffed it in her pocket.

"So . . ." he said, when she still didn't speak. "How about lunch?"

"Fine. Let's go."

Steve sensed something had happened, but did not dare ask for details. Grateful just to be with her, he led the way to the dining room. Jenny ordered wine, something she never did so early in the day, and he thought maybe it would help her mood, so he asked for a whole bottle. By the time they'd finished eating, she was mellowing, and he was able to persuade her to join him for an auction even though she was brooding and had something on her mind. He was going to grasp every moment he could, in hopes of making up for losing his cool the way he had in the clinic. Jenny, he knew, was not going to be pressured into anything, would not respond to heavy moves. He had to take it slowly, easily.

It was nearly five when the farewell party ended. Jenny wanted time alone and brusquely told Steve she'd see him at dinner and headed back to her cabin. Alarmed that Carla was still not there, and, from all appearances had not *been* there, she immediately called the infirmary.

"Miss Sutton is fine," the nurse answering the phone assured Jenny. "We're just keeping her here to be on the safe side. The doctor thinks she should stay till we arrive in Amsterdam, then he'll have her transported directly to the airport by ambulance."

"But I'd like to see her," Jenny argued. "I haven't talked to her since the accident."

"Of course, but she's sleeping again right now. How about after dinner? She'll need clothes for her trip home. If you could bring them by, with her toilet articles, I know she'd appreciate it."

Jenny said she'd be happy to, hung up the phone, and gathered the things she would need.

Then she sat down to cry, hopefully for the last time. *Damn him.* She pounded on her knees with her fists. *Damn him*, why couldn't he have waited? Sure, it would have hurt later to find out the truth, but if she'd had that one last time with him, even if it were only a lie, then at least she could've gone home with happy memories. And wasn't that what this whole *Love Boat* thing was about? To live in a *dream*?

"To hell with it!" she said aloud, forcing herself to come out of her misery. There was one last evening left, and she was going to have a good time. After all, Steve wasn't so bad. Maybe, when she got over feeling like such a fool over Kirk, they might find the beginnings of a relationship . . . though she doubted she would lend her heart again for a long, long time.

Taking Carla's overnight bag with her, Jenny put on a cheerful face for dinner. All around, everyone was celebrating their last night together by exchanging addresses, phone numbers, promising to stay in touch.

When everyone began to leave, Steve hopefully asked, "How about going with me to the farewell show the cruise staff is putting on?"

"I'll have to meet you there," she said, anxious to be on her way. "I'm going to see Carla now."

"Want me to come along?"

Jenny shook her head and hurried off before he could follow.

Carla squealed happily at the sight of her. They embraced and hugged and cried, then Jenny wanted assurance she was truly all right.

"A bit sore, and this ankle hurts like hell sometimes, but other than that, I'm okay. Just grateful it wasn't worse. I don't remember much of anything except falling, but they say you tied the rope around me. Thank God you knew how! Me—I can't keep the laces on my sneakers tied!"

"I owe you thanks, too," Jenny was quick to point out. "It's all foggy, but I seem to remember how you kept me from rolling off that ledge when I didn't realize what had happened."

Then, eyes narrowing suddenly as the vision came back to her of how Carla had so deliberately headed out on the ice, she could not resist accusing, "You were crazy to do what you did, Carla. No man is worth killing yourself over, and—"

"*What?*" Carla hooted at once, and stared at her in

wonder. "You actually thought I was trying to kill myself?"

"You weren't?" Jenny gasped.

"No!" Carla stared at her in wonder. "It was like I said, I wanted something to take home, a memory of Norway. We went ashore in Bergen, but from then on it was drinking, gambling, making what I so stupidly thought was *love*! I just had this crazy, wild feeling inside that if I could go to the glacier, really see it, *feel* the intensity of it, that maybe, just *maybe* I wouldn't feel like such a fool."

Jenny was relieved but persisted. "When you said what you did about how if you fell, you might be reincarnated, well, I thought the worst."

Carla waved away her fears. "Hey, I was letting some of the bitterness out. Oh, it's still there, all right. Probably always will be. Especially when I get the next credit card statement!" She rolled her eyes, then forced a smile. "But I can't worry about that. I mean, we could've both got killed back there, and we didn't, and life is going to go on and I'm going to look forward, not backward.

"And you were so right, Jenny," she rushed on, reaching out to clasp her hands. "About so many things. I wish I knew men the way you do, but I'm learning. I won't be so stupid ever again. I'm going to be smart, like you."

At that, Jenny bitterly scoffed, "Hey, don't look to me as your mentor in the romance department, Carla. I've learned a few things on this cruise myself."

Carla blinked, shook her head, not understanding. "What do you mean? That officer, Kirk Moen, he's adorable. I noticed you were acting kind of strange the morning of the accident, but I didn't think it was anything serious. I mean, he's so crazy about you, and—"

"Stop!" Jenny held up her hands in protest, blinking back fresh tears. "It's over."

"But why?" she gasped. "He's wonderful, and—"

"Carla, you still don't understand, do you? This might as well be Disneyland for all the reality that exists on this ship. Kirk was using me, like Russ used you, only in a different way, and—" She could not go on, knew if she didn't get out of there right that minute she was going to start bawling. Getting to her feet, she said, "Look, I'm going to leave now. You get some rest. I'll be back early in the morning to help you dress, ride with you to the airport. Get some sleep."

She was almost to the door when Carla called, "Hey, I don't know what happened between you two, and maybe it's none of my business, but in my book, the guy's a real hero."

Jenny turned to gape at her and echo, stunned, "*Hero*? What are you talking about?"

It was Carla's turn to gasp. "You mean you don't know?"

"Know *what*?" Jenny took a few hesitant steps toward the bed.

"Kirk is the one who saved our lives. I woke up as we were being unloaded off the helicopter, and I heard one of the pilots telling somebody all about it, how Officer Kirk Moen risked his life to crawl out on that ice and drop a rope down to you to tie around me, then he helped pull us out. Didn't you know?" She searched her face for some sign that she did.

Jenny could only stare at her in wonder. Now the pieces of the puzzle were starting to fit together—how Steve had been so reluctant to discuss any of the details of the rescue, the way he'd steered her quickly away from anyone who'd attempted to talk about it that day, saying "It's over, forget it, don't dwell on it." She herself had not taken the time to discuss it with the doctor or the nurses, wanting only to leave the infirmary.

"How could you *not* know?"

Then the explosion came. "Because, damn it," she clenched her fists, "I asked Steve who pulled us out, and he said it was just somebody on the rescue team. He kept it all from me, and I didn't take time to figure it out for myself. I thought that was Kirk's voice calling to me, and—Damn it!" She cursed again.

"Well, it *was* Kirk," Carla confirmed. "I'm going to write him to thank him. I wish I could see him to thank him in person, but when I mentioned that to the nurse, she said she'd try to get hold of him but not to count on anything. The officers go into high gear when they're winding down a cruise."

The image of Kirk and the blonde flashed, and Jenny sadly murmured, "Oh, they find time for things they really want to do."

"If you see him, tell him thanks for me."

Jenny was no longer listening. She was on her way out. Fury such as she had never known was boiling through her veins. She did not know who that girl was who she'd seen with Kirk, and, for the moment, did not care. Maybe he'd picked her up on the rebound. Maybe she didn't mean a thing to him, like he said of the others. Or maybe he'd lied the whole time. No matter. He had been there. He had cared enough to risk his life to save hers, and that's what *did* matter, and she was going to have her say. She was, by God going to confront him, thank him, and let him know that for whatever it was worth, she *did* care. And if the little blonde didn't like it, so be it!

She rushed to the other end of the ship, to the officers' section, walked right through the forbidding door to pound on Kirk's. There was no response. She looked at her watch. Nearly ten. Was he working? Or was he in there with that blonde making love the way he'd made love to *her*? She knocked again. Louder.

The next door opened. Officer Ingebretsen came out. He looked at her uncertainly, then said, "He's not there, Miss Denton."

"Do you know where he is?"

"He could be anywhere. It's a busy time."

She pushed by him, made her way out and up to the bridge. The door into that was locked from the inside, and she pounded furiously. An officer came to ask what she wanted, then told her Officer Moen was not around. Like Ingebretsen, he had no idea where she might find him.

Jenny was getting frantic. She *was* frantic. No way was she getting off the ship in Amsterdam, or anywhere else, till she saw Kirk, talked to him, thanked him for saving her life—and also told him he was crazy if he thought she just didn't have the courage to love him! She *did*. And now, by God, she was willing to fight for him, too. How easily, she laughed to herself, she'd merely turned and walked away from finding Bryan with Linda.

She headed for the engine room. She was just stepping onto an elevator when Steve rushed up out of nowhere to cry cheerily, "Hey, there you are! I was looking for you, and—"

Jenny pressed the button to freeze the elevator with one hand, while pointing at him in fury with the other. "You lied to me, Steve Gentry!" she cried, oblivious to the others on the elevator who were listening and staring. "You knew all along Kirk was there helping with the rescue, didn't you?"

He could not meet her blazing glare; instead, dropped his head, mumbled, "It could've been great for us, Jenny. I wanted you to see that, and—"

She released the button. The doors closed. She stared straight ahead, not caring about the other passengers. When she reached the bottom deck, she hurried on her way, running to the big steel doors leading to the bowels of the ship.

It was locked.

She pounded furiously, and within a few seconds, a curious officer peered out at her.

"Officer Moen!" she demanded. "I have to see him. *Now.*"

He proceeded to tell her that was not possible. "We have a problem with one of the boilers. He's all the way in the back with the engineers, and—"

She gave the door a shove, knocking the officer back and took off running.

"Hey, you can't go down there!" he yelled.

Jenny kept on going, scooting around machinery, side-stepping crewmen who stared at her in astonishment. She reached the steel catwalk that overlooked the maze of equipment, and then she saw him. He was standing with a group of other officers, and their attention was focused on a big ugly boiler. She cupped her hands around her mouth and called his name. He could not hear her above the clamor of the engines.

She climbed down the narrow ladder carefully, making herself go slowly so she wouldn't fall. Then, just as she stepped down to the floor, he turned and saw her. She broke into a run.

"You saved my life!" She fought to be heard when she reached him to stare up at his incredulous eyes. "It was you, and I didn't know till Carla told me! And I was coming to see you anyway, but you were with that . . . that woman!" She could not keep the rage down at *that* point and screamed, "Damn you, Kirk Moen! I love you! And you don't need her or anybody else, and there's just no way I want to be a passing ship in the night, and—"

"Not here!" he shouted then, very aware that the other officers were enjoying every minute of the unusual scene.

He took her hand, pulled her along, both of them scrambling up the ladder as fast as they dared.

At last they were outside, then in the elevator, wedged in with stacks of suitcases and steamer trunks, with crew members looking, listening. Kirk and Jenny could only stare at each other in silent appraisal.

Finally, they were outside, on the deck, and Kirk drew her into his arms as he sternly said, "Now it's your turn to listen. That woman is my cousin. She came on board in Oslo. And I don't want us to be like ships that pass in the night, either, because dreams *can* become reality, if you dare to open your heart to love . . . to *me*."

She wrapped her arms around his neck, reveling in the closeness, the feeling that his love closed about her to shield from every doubt she ever had. "I do love you, Kirk, and we can make a world together. I know we can."

He held her away from him to look down at her face in adoration. "*Jeg elske deg,* my darling. I love you—in any language."

Their lips met in a kiss of avowal for a love that would not pass like ships in the night.

And then there was only the soft night wind and the timeless eternal sea and the glittering stars above . . . where it had all begun.

It was, for Jenny and Kirk, an ocean of dreams come true.

SHARE THE FUN . . .
SHARE YOUR NEW-FOUND TREASURE!!

You don't want to let your new books out of your sight? That's okay. Your friends can get their own. Order below.

No. 33 A TOUCH OF LOVE by Patricia Hagan
Kelly seeks peace and quiet and finds paradise in Mike's arms.

No. 34 NO EASY TASK by Chloe Summers
Hunter is wary when Doone delivers a package that will change his life.

No. 35 DIAMOND ON ICE by Lacey Dancer
Diana could melt even the coldest of hearts. Jason hasn't a chance.

No. 36 DADDY'S GIRL by Janice Kaiser
Slade wants more than Andrea is willing to give. Who wins?

No. 37 ROSES by Caitlin Randall
It's an inside job & K.C. helps Brett find more than the thief!

No. 38 HEARTS COLLIDE by Ann Patrick
Matthew finds big trouble and it's spelled P-a-u-l-a.

No. 39 QUINN'S INHERITANCE by Judi Lind
Gabe and Quinn share an inheritance and find an even greater fortune.

No. 40 CATCH A RISING STAR by Laura Phillips
Justin is seeking fame; Beth helps him find something more important.

No. 41 SPIDER'S WEB by Allie Jordan
Silvia's quiet life explodes when Fletcher shows up on her doorstep.

No. 42 TRUE COLORS by Dixie DuBois
Julian helps Nikki find herself again but will she have room for him?

No. 43 DUET by Patricia Collinge
Adam & Marina fit together like two perfect parts of a puzzle!

No. 44 DEADLY COINCIDENCE by Denise Richards
J.D.'s instincts tell him he's not wrong; Laurie's heart says trust him.

No. 45 PERSONAL BEST by Margaret Watson
Nick is a cynic; Tess, an optimist. Where does love fit in?

No. 46 ONE ON ONE by JoAnn Barbour
Vincent's no saint but Loie's attracted to the devil in him anyway.

No. 47 STERLING'S REASONS by Joey Light
Joe is running from his conscience; Sterling helps him find peace.

No. 48 SNOW SOUNDS by Heather Williams
In the quiet of the mountain, Tanner and Melaine find each other again.

No. 49 SUNLIGHT ON SHADOWS by Lacey Dancer
Matt and Miranda bring out the sunlight in each other's lives.